MW00760378

1-4-3 Means
I Love You

CLARISSA!

Best Wishes ☺

1-4-3 Means I Love You

Jon Ballard

CNC Publishing, Inc.

Manufactured in the United States of America
Library of Congress Catalog Card Number: 98-94837
ISBN: 0-9668850-0-7
Cover design: Pearl & Associates
Book design and production: Tabby House

CNC Publishing, Inc.
4577 Gunn Highway, Suite 209
Tampa, FL 336624
http://www.booksforall.com

For Helen, Tommy, Corrie,
Kevin and Maria

1

*W*E WEREN'T ABOUT TO LEAVE the Michael Bolton concert until it was over. This man had been nice enough to help bring us together again, so we owed him at least that much. As the concert was ending, his stage manager asked if we would stop backstage for a minute before we left. We accepted without hesitation.

"I hope that you guys can finally be happy together," Michael was saying as we entered his dressing room.

"You helped make it a time that neither of us will ever forget, Michael. I never dreamed it would work out like this. Thanks so much for your help," Gabriella said.

"Mr. Bolton, I'd like to thank you for helping with this little scheme that my daughter and Gabriella cooked up. It was very thoughtful of you."

"Jack, how could I refuse these women. I wouldn't have a fan left if I didn't do something and word got out. You know what I mean?"

"I learned a long time ago that women hold all the cards." We all just laughed.

We talked for a few more minutes and then said our good-byes. Michael had to leave on a plane that night to get ready for another concert in Denver the following evening.

Gabriella and I had finally been reunited and had a million things to catch up on. What had started almost five years ago was all coming together for me. I never dreamed that I'd be with this woman again or be doing what I'm doing now.

After graduating from the University of Alabama, I took a job as an accountant for small businesses. One of my clients turned out to be laundering drug money through his car washing business. Soon, he was asking me to do more work for him, and for a few of his friends, too. What I discovered was a very large drug operation in South Florida. More than half a billion dollars was going through these businesses monthly. I was becoming more and more involved in the whole thing and it was driving me crazy. Sure, I was making lots of money, but how many people was I killing for this money?

My conscience finally got to bothering me so bad that I decided to go to the police with what I knew. They referred me to the FBI, which I found out later had been watching the whole operation, and they made me a deal that I couldn't refuse.

During the next year, I helped convict thirty-two men on various drug laws and two on murder charges. I never thought that it would take as long as it did; the legal system is a mess. I also had to be kept in hiding during this whole time and that got old fast. But these guys would have done anything to keep me quiet, including murder.

When it finally ended, I had a new name and was moved to Central Florida to begin a new career at Tampa Technical Institute. I never dreamed I'd be teaching college. I could have done a million other things besides teaching college. Actually, it turned out to be the most rewarding thing that could have happened to me.

For me, teaching was exciting. Being able to watch people grow and learn, and to feel that I had a small part in shaping their lives, was very fulfilling. The interesting thing is that I was growing and learning, too. Money was never an issue. I would have taught for nothing if I didn't have to pay my bills.

This was also when I met Gabriella. She was in a class I was teaching right after I arrived on campus. From the beginning, I knew she was special. Everything about her was perfect, including the dark hair that touched her shoulders, and those big brown eyes that seemed to trap me from the beginning. When she smiled, she caused me to lose my train of thought, no matter how deep I was in a conversation. At first we were friends and then became very close. We would meet after class, and try to solve each other's problems. We never considered our relationship anything more than just friendship.

After her classes with me ended, I didn't see very much of Gabriella. She became involved with another man and they moved in together.

One evening, about a year later, I was having a drink at the Good Time Charlie's lounge near campus when she came in. I hadn't realized how much I missed talking to her. We spent a long time just catching up with each other's lives. She was still as beautiful as I remembered. We met again a few days later and continued our conversation. Somewhere in the conversation, I fell in love with her. Just like that. I couldn't explain it to her or anyone else. It just happened. I could tell she was attracted to me, but I had no idea whether she felt the same as I did and I surely wouldn't ask. We began seeing more and more of each other and it was obviously becoming difficult for her. She was still living with that guy and had told me on several occasions that she still loved him. I managed to tell her how I felt and she didn't know which way to turn.

Several months later, after Gabriella and I again had been out having a few drinks, I was returning to my house and noticed a strange car parked at the end of the street. There were two men sitting in it. One was smoking a cigarette and the other seemed to be sleeping. I drove to the back of the house and quietly entered, leaving the lights off. The house was torn to pieces. I left immediately and called my contact at the FBI. Somehow the drug dealers had found me and my life in Tampa was over as quickly as it had started. Thirty minutes later I was on a plane.

I ended up in Colorado with another new name and address. I began teaching at the University of Colorado in Colorado Springs. I missed Gabriella very much, but I couldn't contact her for fear that she might be hurt or that those guys would use her to find me. In fact, the feds forced me to lose all contact with her. It hurt worse than I had ever imagined anything could. In my mind, I would try to justify the separation with the fact that it would be better for her. When I left without a word, she was having a terrible time with the guilt-thing anyway, so I imagined that it worked out for the best.

I found out later that it was just as hard on Gabriella as it was for me. She became more and more lost without me. She tried every way she knew to find out what had happened to me. First she tried to locate me through my daughter, Connie, but she had been moved also. Then Gabriella hired a detective to hunt me down. Gabriella did get close through a private investigator in Washington who told her that I was somewhere in Colorado. I guess that was enough information for Gabriella. She moved to Denver and started looking for me.

Completely by accident, she had gone to the airport to fly home for the holidays at the same time my daughter had flown into Denver for a visit with me. They ran into each other and Gabriella's search was over. Connie and I had planned to attend a Michael Bolton concert during her visit so that's where she and Gabriella conspired to have us meet again. Connie and Gabriella even contacted Michael Bolton and got him involved. I was unaware of any of this and got the surprise of my life at the concert. Before he started to play a song called "Missing You Now," he said, "This song is for Jack and Gabriella. I hope they can finally be together." As he began to sing the song, a spotlight came on at the end of the aisle where I was sitting. There in the light stood the most beautiful woman I had ever known and I couldn't even move. She was smiling and crying at the same time. I tried to walk towards her, but I couldn't make my legs move. My heart had stopped momentarily along with every other part of my body. Gabriella began to move towards me, and I finally gained some composure and started toward her. We met somewhere in the light and were finally together. She jumped into my arms. Everyone there began to applaud. That's the last I remember of the crowd. She was in my arms, and I would never let her go again.

We finally made our way back to our seats, and I think we listened to the rest of the concert as we held each other and smiled, or cried, or just looked at one another, still in disbelief. And of course, the rest is history.

2

GABRIELLA, ARE YOU READY to go home?" I asked, kind of jokingly.
"Are you kidding or what. It better not take more than ten minutes to get there or we'll be on the side of the road for the night. By the way, how's your back seat?"

"Five minutes at the most. Is that quick enough?"

"No. But I guess it will have to do."

"Do you think you're ready to spend the rest of your life with me now?"

"Jack, you'll never get away from me again. Period."

We made it to my house in record time and were out of the car just as quickly. I was still in shock that we were finally together. The love I thought lost was here with me. I was sure I had died and gone to heaven.

"Jack, I'm so nervous and excited and happy. Are we really finally together?"

"Let's see," I said as I pulled her close to me.

I put my arms around her waist and we kissed as if it were the first time. We kissed each other like two young kids searching for a new life together. We became one person then, never to be separated.

She pulled away from me only far enough to speak, "Jack, do you have a CD player anywhere here?"

"Sure." What could she possibly want with a CD player right now?
"It's right over there on top of the TV," pointing at the same time in the general direction.

"Perfect," she said as she pulled away from me. She walked over to her purse, pulled out a CD, and put it in the player.

"Gabriella, do we have to listen to that now?"

"Yes. I bought you this CD for this very moment. I knew eventually I'd find you. This had to be our first song alone together. Now, come over here," she ordered.

I walked over to her and put my arms around her. We kissed as the music began to play.

"Darling, this is our new favorite song. I know you've heard it before, but not like this."

It was a song with Kenny G and Peblo Brison called "By The Time This Night Is Over." Gabriella was right. I had heard the song before, but never like this.

"The stars are going to shine on two lovers in love. From now on everything is going to shine for us. I love you, Jack, or whatever your name is," she said. I knew she meant every word of it.

Her eyes were shining, with tears beginning to form in them. She was smiling and crying at the same time. It was all I could do to hold my own tears back.

"Gabriella, I've loved you from the beginning and I always will."

We kissed again and held each other very close. No one or thing would ever separate us again. I wanted to be inside this woman's very soul and she was going to make it happen very soon.

"Jack, would you mind if I took a shower real quick?"

"Since I know there's only one door and you'll be back, I guess it'll be all right."

So far I had managed to hide how nervous I was. It had been such a long time since we had been together that is was like the first time. My heart was beating out of control already and she was still in the shower. This night was going to be wonderful, no matter what happened.

After what seemed like hours, she came out of the bathroom wearing only a towel. She looked so beautiful. The towel covered just enough of her that I had to use my imagination to undress her the rest of the way. The light from the bathroom shone on her from behind and still her eyes were shining. She looked like an angel. I was sure God had sent her to me. I wanted her so desperately, but I didn't want to ever forget the way she looked as she stood there in her towel. Her beauty was locked in my head forever.

"Jack. What are you smiling at?"

"Gabriella, in case I haven't told you lately, I love you. Please come to me. I can't stand this any longer."

She walked over to me and I lowered her to the bed. After a few minutes, I had somehow managed to take off my clothes and was holding her as if I thought she might get away. She still had the towel wrapped around her while we were kissing and becoming comfortable with the idea that we were together. I rose up and pulled away the towel. I stopped breathing momentarily from the beauty I had just exposed.

"Gabriella, don't ever say a word when I tell you how beautiful you are. I can't imagine anyone being more beautiful than you."

That night we became one again. No one would ever take that away from us. We fell asleep after telling each other many secrets that two people always tell each other when these moments happen.

"Gabriella, I hope you never get tired of me."

"Never."

3

*W*e hadn't even begun to think about what the future might bring for us. The last two weeks we had spent just getting to know each other all over again. She was just as warm and passionate as I remembered. I can't believe that I almost gave her up. Sometimes we do things we consider to be in everyone's best interest, that only end up being the wrong decision. I couldn't have been any happier the way things worked out.

Somewhere in the middle of all this, I knew I would have to make the call I dreaded the most. I was sure the FBI would want to move me again and I really loved it here in Colorado. I was also aware that these guys that were hunting me might have been watching Gabriella and could be here soon. The call had to be made and I knew exactly what would happen. My consolation was that, no matter what, Gabriella would be with me. I could handle any situation as long as I knew she would be by my side.

"Steve, we need to talk as soon as possible."

"Is there a problem that we need to handle right this minute, Jack?"

"So far there isn't, but it could if we don't do something. Could we meet somewhere in the next couple of days?"

"How about the Denver airport on Thursday. Say about noon. That restaurant we had lunch at when you arrived. Sound good?"

"Sounds great, Steve. See you then."

I hung up the phone and went to speak with Gabriella. "Gabriella, you know we might have to move again, and I'm not looking forward to that. I'll bet you're tired of moving around, too, but it would be for our safety."

"Jack, I've spent a long time trying to find you, and now that I've done that, nothing else matters. I'll go anywhere you go, anytime. You don't even have to ask."

"I was sure that was what you would say, but I needed to hear it. It really is for our safety. Besides, we can be happy anywhere. I promise you that."

"Do you have any idea where they might send us?"

"You can't imagine how good that sounds to me—'Where they might send us.' I never thought that I'd hear that, much less be asked that by you. Honestly, I have no idea. They make all the arrangements and I find out when I get there. Now they will have to make them for two. Period."

She just smiled. I put my arms around her and we kissed. How I could have existed without her all this time was beyond me. I was still somewhere in the clouds and nothing else mattered but being with her.

"I love you, Gabriella."

"I'm sure you know by now that I love you too."

We became one again.

On Thursday, we left early for Denver so that we could see the sun rise over the mountains as we made the short trip from Colorado Springs. About halfway there, I made a left turn onto one of the many side roads that leads to one of the lodges in the area.

"Gabriella, have you had a chance to visit any of the lodges while you've been here?"

"Are you kidding? All I've done since I moved here is look for you and work. I was always on the road visiting each college campus in and around Denver. If there was a lodge, I drove right by it."

"I'm sorry. I wish I could have made it easier for you."

"Don't be. We're together now, and that's all that matters. Where are we going, anyway?"

"You'll see. It isn't very far."

As I drove up to the lodge and parked the car, I noticed that she was crying. I was sure it wasn't out of sadness, but something had to be wrong. "What's wrong, honey? I didn't say anything, did I?"

"Jack, I love you. I'm sorry, it just happened and I couldn't help it. I have just imagined so many times, how exciting it would be for us to be together and not have to leave each other. I'm just happy. Don't worry."

I leaned over and held her very close. I understood just what she meant. This was still all new to us. I kissed her gently and we got out of the car.

I waited at the car door pretending to have trouble locking it as she walked ahead toward the door of the lodge.

"Jack, what are you doing?" she said as she turned to look for me.

"I'm still amazed at how beautiful you really are, and I just wanted to see you walking off." She still took my breath away. I wanted to go straight to the desk and get a room.

"Get up here right now, mister," she said smiling.

As I approached her, she took a snowball and threw it at me. For the next few minutes we had a snowball fight. I won.

I asked the waitress to seat us at a table by a window looking out at the mountains. It was still fairly dark outside, but if we were lucky, the sun would come up at just the right spot. We ordered our breakfast. While we were waiting we talked about the people who were already making their way to the ski lifts.

"Jack, do you know how to ski? I mean, have you learned how to ski since you've been here. I remember in one of your classes that you said you tried it, but you couldn't stand up."

"Funny you should ask. No, I still can't stand up. How about you?"

"I guess we'll just have to learn how together. I wonder if it's possible to wear skis to bed?" she said and I saw that mischievous look in her eyes that I remembered so well from our times together in Florida.

"Might be fun to try it. Maybe on the way back tonight."

Our breakfast came very fast and so we began to eat. I was starving and dug into mine like it might be my last.

"Jack. Look," she said pointing out the window.

The sun had just peeked through the clouds between two of the mountains. It was a bright orange and reflected right off the snow. I can't remember anything so beautiful. We sat there a few minutes, and watched as it changed colors. Reflecting across the mountains, hitting first the snow, then the trees. It was breathtaking.

"Jack, come sit beside me."

I sat in the chair next to hers and she leaned back, putting her head close to me. I wrapped my arms around her and held her close. This is how life should be, I thought. I know she felt my heart beating against her back. I couldn't help it. I wondered if this feeling I had for her would ever change. I forgot all about breakfast. I kissed her gently, and she smiled.

About an hour later, we were back on the road again making our way to Denver. We arrived at the airport about 11:00 A.M. We walked through the place arm in arm, just enjoying everything and everybody.

"Jack, that's where I ran into Connie."

"Do you realize it might have been a long time before you found me if you two hadn't run into one another here?"

"We were meant to be together. Someone higher up was watching after us." She steered me toward the exact spot and said, "Right here, Jack." She threw her arms around me and gave me a kiss.

Just before noon, we made our way to the restaurant where we were to meet Steve. We sat down and ordered drinks while we waited. Before our drinks arrived, he came up smiling.

"It's good to see you again, Jack," Steve said, extending his hand for me to shake.

"Hi, Steve, you still look like an accountant to me," I said laughing.

"Steve, I'd like you to meet Gabriella Newman."

"You're kidding. How'd you ever find her?"

"I didn't. She found me."

"I'm sorry, nice to finally meet you, Gabriella."

"Nice to meet you, Steve. You did a good job of hiding him. It was by total accident that I did find him."

"Would you believe she ran into Connie at the airport a couple of weeks ago. Gabriella was leaving for Florida and Connie was coming to see me."

We spent the next few minutes explaining how we had finally come together, laughing and enjoying the story.

"Sounds like you guys were meant to be together, Gabriella."

"That's what I keep telling him."

"This really changes things, Jack. I had hoped that we could convince you to do some work for us. I ran across something that is going down at the agency and thought you might be interested."

"This does change some things. I'm never going anywhere again without Gabriella."

Gabriella couldn't resist Steve's proposition and asked, "What is it, Steve?"

"It doesn't matter now. We can't do it the way things are now—it would be too dangerous. I'm not sure Jack would have wanted to do it anyway. I'll go back to the bureau and get you guys relocated."

"Thanks Steve. I'm sure you understand that I just want to spend the rest of my life somewhere with this woman."

But Gabriella couldn't leave it alone. "Jack, you should at least hear what he had in mind. This doesn't sound like you at all. I don't want you changing just because I'm here. Tell us, Steve."

"You might as well tell us, Steve. She won't leave you alone 'til you do."

"OK, but it won't work now. I want you to understand that up front."

"No problem. I just wanted to save you a lot of grief. She's very persistent."

"OK. There's this little university town in Southern California that is a drug haven. I was going to see if I could get you to go down there and help break it up. It's bigger than the one in Florida."

"What makes you think I would have done it, Steve? I'm in enough trouble because of the last time I got involved with this stuff."

"It's cocaine, and it's going straight to the kids."

"Jack, we could do it," I heard Gabriella saying.

"Gabriella, don't think for one minute we're going to get involved in this deal at all. We just got back together, and that's the way I want to keep it. Steve, tell her it wouldn't work," I said almost loud enough for the whole restaurant to hear.

"Jack's right. It might have worked if we had sent him in alone, but we would have a hell of a time with both of you out there. I'll just find you guys a nice quiet place and let you be happy," Steve said as I sat nodding my head in agreement.

* * *

I had a feeling that this conversation wasn't over with. I knew that Gabriella was going to start using some of my own psychology on me to try to change my mind and I would be in trouble. The thing I was sure she would use first was something that had done successfully when we were going through some other difficult times—the silent treatment. I remembered when we had been seeing each other for about three months and she had to choose between her boyfriend and me. I appeared to be on the losing end because she seemed to be doing things to me in an attempt to end our relationship, such as not talking to me anymore. I had already told her that I loved her and she had told me the same thing, and in my mind, once that happened, there was nothing that was going to keep us apart. But after a week of silence, I caught up with her as she was about to leave the parking lot at her job.

"Gabriella, unless you really don't care anything at all about me, I think you should listen to me for five minutes," I remember telling her.

"Jack, it won't make any difference. This has to stop." Her chilling words came back to me.

"In other words, you've made up your mind to stay where you're at and there's nothing I can do."

"Jack, I can't hurt him and I want to make it work. I'm sorry, but that's all I can do."

"Gabriella, if you can tell me that you don't have any feelings for me, then I'll leave you alone. Completely."

"That's not fair, Jack. You know I do."

"I once saw a movie that could help you with your problem. Want to hear?"

"Why not. I'm sure you'd tell me anyway," she said in a tone that wasn't what I was used to.

"Never mind. This isn't working. I need to get away from here," I said and began to walk away.

"Jack, I'm sorry. This just isn't easy. Please tell me what you were going to say," she said as she grabbed my arm.

"OK, Gabriella, but this is it. After I've had my say, I'm out of here. This hasn't been easy on me either."

"Jack, please!"

"The movie was about this doctor who gave up his practice because a little girl he had operated on had died. He went to India searching for some sort of inner peace. Well, he ended up in a small village. It was very poor and, of course, there was no permanent doctor. He refused to help this nurse that runs a small clinic and nothing she can do will change his mind. But finally she said something to him that eventually changed his mind. She said, 'There are only three things that you can do in this world. Run away all your life, be a spectator, or change what is wrong.' Gabriella, I can't make you decide what to do about us, but I do know this. You've already tried two of these things. I love you," I said as I turned and walked away.

* * *

In retrospect, I'm not sure if or how that helped her choose between two men, but for whatever reason, we're together now. I didn't want anything to come between us again and I was braced for her response to Steve's conversation.

Suddenly she said, "Jack, remember what you told me one time about the doctor. Something about running away all your life, being a spectator, or changing what is wrong."

"Gabriella, this is different. Besides that, Steve already said that it wouldn't work."

"OK, we'll talk about it later."

I knew the discussion wasn't over with, but I was glad that she was giving in now. I didn't want to talk about it anymore in front of Steve. Turning to him, I said, "See what you can do about getting us relocated. Classes start up soon and I want to make the move before then."

"No problem, Jack. I'll be back in touch with you in a couple of days. Gabriella, it really is OK. You guys deserve to be happy."

"I understand. That's what I really want, too," she said.

"It was nice to see you both. I'll be in touch real soon," Steve said. He got up, made his exit, and we were alone.

"I hope you're not upset with me, Gabriella."

"We'll talk about it later, Jack. Don't worry. I'm too happy right now about *us* to be upset about anything."

"Are you hungry?"

"Not really, but I can eat if you are."

We had a light lunch before we left the airport, then we made our way back to the car about an hour later and headed back to Colorado Springs.

"Jack, could we stay at that lodge tonight?" she said with that look that I could never turn down.

"Sure. I guess you want to learn how to ski tonight," I said smiling at her. She looked so content sitting next to me. I hoped that she knew how happy I was. She leaned over and put her arm around me and kissed me on the cheek. I began to exceed the speed limit.

We checked into the lodge, went to the room, and made love for several hours. I still couldn't believe we were together.

"You want to go for a walk?"

"Sounds like fun to me, but no skis. OK?"

We took a lift up to one of the small peaks that was used for beginning skiers.

We walked over to one of the lookout points and held each other as we gazed at the beauty of the mountains.

"I love you, Gabriella. You've made me very happy."

"I tried not to love you, Jack, but I couldn't help myself. I'm really glad I lost the war I had with myself. I'm happier now than I've ever been in my life," she said and we kissed passionately.

"Jack, you're going to get into trouble if you don't stop kissing my neck and you know it," she said playfully.

"Ever made love in the snow?" I said kidding with her.

"Not 'til now. What about the people?"

We looked around and there were no people. I took her hand and we walked off the path to a quiet spot. We almost froze to death, but it was exciting. Too bad we didn't have a camera.

That evening we lay in the bed holding each other as we fell asleep. She was so warm. Our bodies fit together like they had been molded that way. I dreamed about her as I slept. I was awakened, however, by the sound of her voice.

"Jack, I can't sleep. Are you sleeping?"

"Do you realize that you woke me up in the middle of a very exciting dream about you? What happens if I can't start it up again?" I said, smiling to her.

"I'll finish it for you. Will that work?"

"Enough said. Why can't you sleep?" I knew exactly what it was.

"Jack, I really think we should try and stop those drugs from hurting people. I know you want to just be together, but we will. We'll be working together."

She looked so serious and I knew I was in a no-win situation. I still had to try. "Gabriella, first of all, Steve said the bureau wouldn't go for it. Next, what about marriage, family, and happily ever after? What about that?"

"We can still get married. We might have to wait on the family. Wait a minute. We haven't even talked about this subject yet. How do you know I'd even marry you?" she said, as she poked at my side.

"I had hoped you would, but if you don't want to..." I said and poked out my lip like a child who has been denied something.

"Are you asking?"

"Absolutely."

"Then I will absolutely marry you. But that doesn't change anything. I still think we should try."

I felt tears almost come to my eyes and she saw it, too. "I'm sorry. I know men aren't supposed to do that, but you have made me very happy.

By the way, I'll call Steve and see what he says." Then she began to cry. We held each other and fell back asleep.

* * *

"Steve, I can't change her mind. I hate to admit it, but she's right. We can do it," I heard myself saying into the receiver the next morning.

"Jack, I've already done some checking. I was sure she would convince you. Women always win when they set their minds to it. Gabriella is very beautiful, Jack. You're a lucky guy," Steve continued. "We might be able to do something. We can meet again Monday at the airport. That OK with you?"

"Sure, Steve, what time?"

"Say about three."

"See you then," I said and hung up.

I found Gabriella just getting out of the shower. She had a towel wrapped around her and she was drying her hair. The mirror was all fogged up, so it made for a perfect time to be mischievous. The towel was so easy to get off her. I grabbed it and ran out of the bathroom with Gabriella screaming and running after me. I ran past the bedroom into the living room and hid behind one of the chairs. It became very quiet. I waited and waited. She never came. I slowly made my way back towards the bedroom. I was sure she would be hiding somewhere with some kind of retaliation. I leaned my head through the bedroom door and looked around. I found her on the bed lying on her side, propped up on her elbow. She was smiling and she had that look in her eyes. Her hair was still wet and the sun was reflecting off it as water was running down her shoulders.

"I guess you'll just have to finish drying me off since you stole my towel," she said as her eyes began to sparkle with excitement.

"Hmm...I lost the towel somewhere, but I guess I could find some way to dry you off." I ran and jumped on the bed.

"I love you, Jack. You're not getting tired of me yet, are you?"

"Never," I replied. We made love and it was wonderful. We were becoming more comfortable with each other, and began experimenting with new and exciting ways to please each other.

"You know why making love to you will never get boring for us?" I said.

"Because I'm so good at pleasing you," she said with a smile.

"Absolutely," I replied. "And because we both try to please each other. That's why it will never become boring." I picked her up and carried her to the door of the shower. I kissed her and we got in. "By the way, Steve wants to see us Monday."

"You knew that all this time and you're just now telling me. You're going to pay for this one, mister," she said. And I did. Everyone should have to suffer that way.

4

*W*E ARRIVED LATE FOR OUR MEETING with Steve. As we walked up to the restaurant, he was sitting there having what looked to be a mixed drink, maybe a bourbon and Coke.

"How are you two doing? Glad you finally made it," he said jokingly.

"Sorry, Steve, we just misjudged the time."

"You guys want a drink?" he asked.

"Sure."

After a few minutes the drinks came and Steve began. "I talked with my boss and he says that if you guys will come in for some training, we will work from there. If the training goes as I expect, you will become temporary agents. Does that sound OK to the both of you?"

"How hard is the training? I'm not in very good shape."

Gabriella couldn't resist that one. "Don't listen to him. He's in excellent shape. Do you think we can handle it, Steve?"

"It will be hard, but I'm sure you'll do just fine."

"Well, what do we do next?"

"You need to be at our Denver office one week from today. Will that be enough time for you to make a quiet exit from the college?"

"That should work out fine. I just need time to say a few good-byes and we'll be ready."

"I'm really getting excited about all this," Gabriella said.

"Don't get too excited yet. You might hate me by the time this is over."

"Steve, there was a guy who worked with me while I was in Florida. His name is Gary Stephens, but it could be anything now. They put him under protection at the same time they did me. He could be a big help when we do start this thing. Would you see if you could get him up here?"

"I can't promise you anything, but I'll do some checking," he replied.

We finished our drinks and were about to leave when Steve said, "Are you sure you want to do this? There's still time to bail out."

"We've made up our minds. We'll be there Monday. Will you be there to meet us?" Gabriella asked.

"Sure," he replied. "I'll see you guys then. Don't worry about a thing." We watched as he walked off.

"Well, Gabriella, there's no turning back now."

"We'll be fine, Jack. Just as long as we're together," she said smiling.

"You're truly an amazing woman."

"If I am, you made me that way," she said as we were leaving.

I wasn't really sure how all this was going to turn out, but I was sure that I wanted to share the rest of my life with this woman.

"Jack, I have to call my parents," she said as we were getting in the car. "Can I have them fly out? I think it's time they meet you, and they have no idea that I was here to find you. My sister does, but she's the only one. Could we maybe meet them, say halfway or something. Please?"

I thought to myself that it would be impossible for anyone to turn down this woman and responded immediately. "We'll call them as soon as we get home."

"Jack, I love you," she said and she kissed me. "You're never going to get rid of me, you know?"

"I sure hope not. We're in this to the end."

As we traveled back toward the college she asked about Gary. "How does he fit in all of this? You never mentioned him before."

"He worked for one of the guys that I got convicted. He wasn't involved in the operation, but because he worked for them and was aware of the illegal acts, he would have been arrested along with the rest of them. I got to know him right after I started to do the books for his boss. We played basketball together. We'd go out chasing women and all that stuff. Anyway, I told him what I was doing and arranged for him to work with us. He was a nice guy. I couldn't let him go down with the others."

"Weren't you afraid he might tell his boss?"

"Not the way he used to beat me at basketball. I lost a lot of money to him before I figured out what he was doing." I paused and smiled before continuing. "I'm just kidding. We became very good friends right from the beginning and I just knew he wouldn't. I hope they bring him here with us. I'm sure you'll like him. He's a lot like me, only taller."

"I'm sure I will. He must have really impressed you to take that kind of a risk."

"He's a great guy."

We drove for a while without saying a word. This was that kind of silent time when words aren't necessary and the mind just wonders in sheer contentment. Gabriella was looking out the window, watching the Colorado countryside. My mind was on harder times. I just wanted Gabriella to be safe and with me.

"Would you mind very much if we stopped somewhere so that I can call my parents? I can't wait any longer to tell them about us. Maybe we can stop at the next exit. Please?" Gabriella said loudly, without any kind of warning.

She startled me so badly that I jerked the wheel and had to kind of jump at the steering wheel with my other hand. I quickly gained my composure and remarked, "Gabriella, you scared the shit out of me. I was daydreaming, and, well...you know what I mean. Now what was that you said?"

"Could we stop so I can call my parents? It'll only take a minute. I just have to tell them."

"I'll stop at the next exit. It's only about a mile up the road. Do you think you can wait that long or should I speed up some?" I said, trying to be funny.

"You're gonna pay for that later, mister. Just get me to a phone."

"Yes, general."

I pulled off at the next exit, and entered the first convenience store I saw. "Will this do, my love?"

"It'll only take a minute. Come with me so you can talk to them too."

"OK, I'm coming."

It wasn't long before she had them on the phone. "Hi, Mom. How's everything? No, everything is just fine....Colorado is beautiful. Mom, I don't have much time right now. I found Jack...Jack. You remember, I told you about him. One of my teachers back in Florida. Jack Cannon. I mean Jack Kincaid. Never mind, I'll explain later...yea, that's right. Mom, I'm in love with him and I want you guys to meet him...Yes, Mom, I'm sure...Hi, Dad....Yes, I said I'm in love....No, it's not a little quick. This is the guy I was in love with for a long time...Yes, Dad, I know you're just worried. Dad, I don't have much time. Can you and Mom and maybe Sis fly out to Denver this weekend and meet Jack and me? I know it's short notice, but it's the only time we'll have for awhile....Yes, Dad, it is that important. Dad, we'll even pay for the tickets," she said looking over at me for approval. I just nodded my head. "Dad, try and get a flight coming in on Friday, because we have to be in Denver that day, OK, Dad, you know I wouldn't ask you to do this if it wasn't important...thanks, Dad. I love you. Could I speak to Mom again, please? Bye, Daddy. I love you, Mom. OK. See you Friday. I'll call you Thursday night to find out what time your plane arrives. I love you. Tell Sis I love her. Bye," and she hung up the phone.

"Feel better?"

"Jack, I forgot to let you talk to them. I was so excited, it just...."

I stopped her in mid-sentence. "Gabriella, it doesn't matter. I'll see them Friday and I can talk to them then."

"OK. I can be such a dip-shit some times."

"You might be, but you're *my* dip-shit," I said smiling at her as we walked back to the car, got in, and drove off.

5
Gabriella

Mom and Dad's flight was due in at 7:05 and it was almost that time when we arrived, parked the car, and made our way into the terminal. When we got there, however, we discovered that for some reason the flight had been delayed two hours, so we decided to go get something to eat in town.

As we were walking back to the car, I asked Jack what we had left to do before we had to report to the FBI training center.

"We don't have to worry about any of the furniture, because it was furnished by them. I just have to pack my clothes. The only other thing I have to do is say good-bye to Dan and his family. They were a big help when I needed someone to talk to. He's the one who went to Florida looking for you. Remember?"

"The old Vietnam buddy, right?"

"Right. I'll have to tell you about those days sometime."

He put the key in the passenger door and opened it for me. "Gabriella, it's been a while since I mentioned this, but I still love you," he said as I was about to get in the car.

I put my arms around him and kissed him as if we were going to make love right there in the parking lot. "I love you too, Jack."

He walked around, put the key in his door, and started to open it. Suddenly, there was a loud noise! The first shot must have hit him in the shoulder because he hit the window with the impact. He looked at me as if he couldn't believe he'd been shot. I reached for him across the seat. I couldn't believe what was happening. The second shot hit him somewhere in the back. He immediately fell to the ground. I jumped from the car and ran around to his side. "Jack," I screamed as I approached. He was lying face down on the concrete and I was terrified. "Jack, talk to me," I said as I turned him over and placed his head in my lap. "Someone call an ambulance," I screamed, as people were approaching. I couldn't tell whether he was breathing or not. He was very still and looked so far away. "Jack, please don't die. We have our whole lives to live together," I whispered to him.

After what seemed like hours, the ambulance arrived. I heard the paramedic say, "Miss, you have to let go of him or we won't be able to help him. Miss, please let go." I could hear him, but I couldn't let go.

The other paramedic pulled my arms loose and got me to my feet. "Are you OK? Stand here for a minute while we look at your friend," he ordered.

"Just worry about him. I'm all right now. Please tell me that he's alive," I cried to them.

"He's still alive, miss, but barely. We need to get him to the hospital as soon as possible. Willie, get us a chopper here, pronto."

The helicopter arrived shortly and they loaded Jack in it. I didn't hesitate to climb in the chopper with them. They didn't try to stop me, even if they had it on their minds.

I sat across from the paramedics and held Jack's hand.

"Please hold on Jack. I love you. You can't die. Do you hear me?" I whispered. "Is he going to make it?"

"We're doing all we can. Right now he's holding on. We're only a few minutes from the hospital now. He should make that easy enough."

As we arrived at the landing pad, I saw them wheeling out a gurney to carry him on. The minute we touched down they had him loaded and were headed inside. I could barely keep up. They were screaming all kinds of things that I couldn't understand. They carried him through some doors and one of the nurses told me that this was as far as I could go. I put my hands on the doors and started to cry out of control. Another nurse came to my aid.

"Come over here and sit down, miss. It'll be a little while before we know anything. Can I get you a glass of water or a cup of coffee?"

"Water would be fine, thank you. Maybe some tissue, please."

She returned with a box of tissue and a cup of water. "Here you are, miss."

"I need you to do me a big favor and it's very important. I need Jack's wallet. There's a number I have to call and it's in his wallet. Can you get it for me, please?"

"I'll do what I can. I'll be right back," she said. In a couple of minutes she returned carrying the wallet. "This what you need, miss?"

"Yes, thank you very much. Is there a phone I can use close by?"

"Down at the nurses' station."

"Thank you."

Soon I found the number I was looking for, and found a phone at the nurses' station. "Steve, this is Gabriella. Jack's been shot."

"Gabriella, where are you? Which hospital? Where are you?" he repeated.

"Memorial Hospital in Denver."

"I'll be right there." He had already hung up the phone.

Steve arrived at the hospital in about thirty minutes. I still hadn't heard anything from anyone and was just about to go crazy.

As he approached, I ran to him and started crying all over again. "Steve, it was terrible. I think he may be dead and they won't tell me anything at all."

He put his arms around me and said, "Calm down. I'll see if I can find out anything. I'll be right back."

Steve went to the nurses' station, showed his badge, and asked if they could give him any information on Jack. "I'll go see what I can find out," I heard one of the nurses say. Steve returned to the waiting room where I sat.

"Gabriella, can you tell me anything about what happened? If you don't want to talk about it, I understand."

"All I remember is that he was about to get in the car at the airport and two shots hit him from behind. It all happened so fast. I thought I was having a dream or something. Maybe that officer can tell you more. He was the first one there."

Steve walked to the officer. "I'm Steve Fuller with the FBI. Can you tell me anything about what happened?"

"Mr. Fuller, you'll have to talk to the detectives on the case. All I did was make sure they got him here before it was too late. They are doing all the investigative work. If you want, I'll get one of them here," he said.

"If you would, please. I need to let our office know what is going on," Steve explained.

"Sure thing, Mr. Fuller. This guy one of your agents?"

"Under our protection," he answered.

"Did the nurse get back yet?" Steve asked.

"Not yet," I replied.

"I'll be right back. Want some coffee or anything?"

"I'll have some coffee, black, please."

"Sure thing. Don't worry, Gabriella. As long as we don't hear anything there's still hope. I'll be right back," and he was gone.

I saw him go back to the nurses' station and could hear him getting a little more forceful this time. "I want to know something now! This lady has been here for two hours and you haven't told her anything," I heard him say.

Finally, the nurse that he had originally talked to came back. I couldn't hear what they were saying, but I knew enough to understand that it was serious. Steve returned after a few minutes.

"What is it, Steve? Is he OK? Steve, what's wrong?" I said and began to cry.

"Gabriella, give me a minute and I'll explain what I can. Calm down. Jack is still alive. They are still operating on him. From what I could get from the nurse, the bullets are lodged just below his heart. Very tricky surgery, but he's holding on. She'll tell us as soon as anything happens."

"Oh, shit, Steve. My parents! They're at the airport. We were meeting them there today. They must be worried to death."

"What time was their flight?"

"Around seven, but it was delayed for some reason. Can you have someone find them for me?"

"It shouldn't be any problem. What's your father's name?"

"José Newman. Could you have them get in touch with me here at the hospital?"

"Yea, but I don't think they should come here. It might be best if they fly back home and you see them another time. We don't need any more trouble. They might not be safe. Do you understand?"

"Steve, I need my mother here. She will be so worried. Can they come by for just a few minutes? Please."

"Gabriella, it's not a good idea. The killers could be following your parents. I'll arrange for them a flight home. I'm sorry."

"It's all right. I know you're right. Just have them call me and I'll explain."

"It's the best thing."

"Thanks, Steve."

Hours later, around 4:00 A.M., Jack was still in the operating room. I thought to myself, *It must be a nightmare, and I'll wake up and it will all be better.* He had been shot around 7:30 and was in surgery by 8:00 P.M. That meant eight hours of surgery. I began to cry again and pray at the same time. He had to get better. Now that we were finally together, it couldn't end like this. I loved this man too much.

I thought back to the time that we had first started seeing each other. "Jack, I love my boyfriend and I'll never leave him," I had said many, many times to him.

"Gabriella, I never asked you to leave your boyfriend. I'll take any part of you that I can have," he would say.

I did everything possible to make him stop loving me. I know I hurt him, but, at the time, I was torn between what I felt was right and the desire I had to be with him. There were times I wouldn't even let him kiss me because I felt so guilty about even being with him. I wanted to stop seeing him, and when I would, I only wanted to be with him again. At the time, I was sure Jack and I would never be together and told him so. He would only look at me and say, "Let's just take it one day at a time."

"Gabriella, Jack's out of surgery," I heard Steve saying as I came back to reality. "Gabriella, did you hear me?"

"Is he all right? Can I see him? Where is he? I have to be with him," I was saying, not giving Steve even a chance to explain.

"Calm down. They have just taken him to a room and his condition is still iffy. He'll be in intensive care for a while. They say the next twenty-four to forty-eight hours will be the deciding factor," I heard him say.

What was he talking about? The next twenty-four to forty-eight hours? Intensive care? Might be the deciding factor? Jack had to be all right! "Steve, what is wrong? Are you telling me everything? I just have to know. Will he be all right? Steve. . . ." I began to cry uncontrollably. If I could just stop maybe Steve would explain. Still, I couldn't stop crying.

"Pull yourself together and let me explain what the doctor told me. Are you listening to me, Gabriella?"

"Oh, Steve, I'm better now. Please tell me what's going on," I said through the tears.

"The bullets that he was shot with were designed to shatter once they entered into his body. They did exactly that. The doctors got as much of the fragments out as possible, but feel that there is still more," he was saying as I was still gaining my composure. "There were fragments in his lungs, stomach, spine, and even parts of his heart. They say he's very lucky to be alive at all. Anyway, they felt they had to stop at this point to let him build up his strength. They almost lost him several times."

I began to cry again. "What happens now? He can't die. Please tell me, he's not going to die."

"It's just too early to tell."

"I have to see him, Steve. Please!" I said through my tears.

"I'll see what I can do. Please stop crying. I'm not good at watching women cry. I'll be right back," and he was gone.

I again tried to pull myself together. I couldn't let Jack see me like this even if he wouldn't be aware that I was in the same room with him. This man was such a positive person and he had made me one too. I was sure now that he was going to be all right. Now I just wanted to see him. Period.

Steve returned after a short while and gave me the news I wanted to hear. "Gabriella, you can see him for a few minutes, but that's all. He won't be aware that you are there, but I convinced them that you had to see him. Remember, just a few minutes."

"I'll take what time I can get, Steve. I just want to be with him and let him know I'm here. He must not think he's alone. Not for a minute. Steve, please take me to him."

When I entered the room, the first thought I had was one of all the life this man had in him. He was always so positive and full of happiness. I looked down at Jack and everything seemed to have been drained out of his body. His face was pale, almost white. His eyes were closed, but I could tell they were drawn back in his head and the smile was gone from his face. The amazing thing was that I could still sense the life in his body. Even as near to death as he was, he could take hold of the moment and make people feel alive and good about themselves. I knew he was going to be all right.

"Jack, I'm here and you know I love you. Please hurry up and get better. We have many, many things to do. OK?" I whispered.

"Gabriella, he can't hear you. He's still very heavily sedated. Why don't we come back later," Steve said.

"He's going to be all right, I'm sure of that. I also know that he hears me. You have to understand that we have a love that was destined to be complete and we have just started. Just give me a minute alone with him and we can leave then," I explained. I reached down and held his hand and talked to him again. "Jack, I'll be right here when you wake up. Just tell them you want to see me. I promised you that we'd never be apart again and we won't." I kissed him on the cheek and we left the room.

"Gabriella, I had the luggage you had in the car taken to a motel right next door. We got a room for you there because I was sure you would want to be close. That all right with you?"

"That's perfect. I want to be as close as possible. I plan to be here as long as it takes. Did you put his luggage there too?"

"Yes. Is there something else you need?"

"I really didn't bring much to wear since we only came up here to visit with my parents. I might have to get some more things from my apartment. It's here in Denver and not too far away.

"You can't go anywhere near your apartment or Jack's house. The guy who decided to do this may still be around to make sure his job is done. You have to understand that. Your past is truly your past. You really are a part of his world now. Are you ready for that?"

"I've always been a part of his world. This is just the next step. What do you want me to do?"

"Nothing for now. You just spend as much time as it takes with Jack now. We'll get what we can from your apartment and his house. Once that's done, that part of your life and his will be over," he stated. "By the way, we'll have an agent with you twenty-four hours a day now and someone here at the hospital at all times until we're sure it's safe."

"Thanks, Steve, I don't want any more problems."

"Here's the key to your room, but don't leave until our agent arrives to go with you. I have to leave for a while, but I'll be back later. I've arranged for a bed here at the hospital for you tonight. Just ask the nurses. If I were you, I wouldn't leave before the morning. OK?"

"That's perfect. See you later."

I went back to the waiting room. I suddenly felt very alone. It was now about 4:30 in the morning and I felt myself getting very tired. How could this have happened after all we had been through. It didn't matter except that it just wasn't fair. I mean, this was supposed to be one of those, "And they lived happily ever after" things and now . . . . I thought about something Jack said to me once during our troubled times, "Gabriella, nothing will ever change how I feel about you. You can try to drive me away from you, you can insult me, you can avoid me, and you can leave without saying good-bye, but I will always love you. The good, the bad, and the beautiful. So you might as well quit trying." How did he know? Why did he keep trying even when I was a real shit? God, I love this man.

6

*M*ISS, YOU'LL HAVE TO GET UP NOW. We have people who need to sit down," I heard a nurse saying.

"I'm sorry. Can you tell me what time it is?" The sun was shining through the windows and I knew I must have been asleep for hours.

"It's 10:00 A.M. You slept here quite a while," the nurse said. "We started to wake you earlier, but we decided that you needed the rest."

"Can I see Jack? Is there any change? You should have woke me earlier," I rambled as I ran my fingers through my hair to straighten it, although it really didn't.

"The doctor wants to talk to you before you see him. I'll take you there. Would you like to wash up a bit first?" the nurse asked.

"Please. I must look like a wreck."

"I have to get back to work, but Agent Hunter is here to help you," the nurse said.

I looked over at the chairs across from where we were and saw the slender blonde woman sitting there. She must have been only about 110 pounds and yet she was dressed in what looked like a professional-style suite. She had a badge hanging off her belt. Could this be the agent that Steve said he would send over? She was beautiful and elegant. Big brown eyes highlighted her medium length hair. I never imagined a female agent, especially one that looked like this. "Don't judge people by the first impression. See what's in their heart," Jack used to say in class. So, I must wait and see.

She got up and came over to me. So graceful and easy that I again found myself thinking that she couldn't be an agent. "Hi, I'm Special Agent Cheryl Hunter. Steve sent me over to stay with you," she said pointing to her badge. "I know what you're thinking. Everyone does at first, but I really am."

"So I guess I'm not the first. Sorry, people shouldn't assume."

"Since we're going to be spending some time together, would you mind calling me Cheryl?" she asked.

"Only if you call me Gabriella."

"No problem. Let me take you to where you can freshen up. Would you like to have a cup of coffee?"

"Could I just have a glass of orange juice, please?" I asked as we headed toward the restroom.

"I'll get it while you clean up. If you don't mind, I would appreciate it if you wait in here until I return. You're my responsibility now and I want to keep you safe."

"I guess we better be careful for a while. Thanks, I'll stay here, but please hurry. I want to see Jack as soon as possible."

I looked at myself in the mirror and wondered why Jack always said I was beautiful. I was a total wreck. He must be blind. I threw water on my face, dried it, and put on my usual amount of makeup. Then I ran a brush through my hair. It was as good as it gets.

"Here's your O.J. I thought you might like a doughnut, too." Cheryl had returned as I was fluffing up my hair.

"Thanks, I could use a little something in my stomach. Can you take me to the doctor I'm supposed to talk to?" I asked as I gulped down the juice and the sticky doughnut.

"We'll have to check with the nurse and see which one it is you're supposed to see, but we'll get it done." We went out into the hallway, and spotted a nurse down the hall.

"Gabriella was supposed to talk to a doctor about Jack Cannon." Cheryl asked, "Could you tell us which doctor we're supposed to see?"

"I'll check," the nurse said as she began to look on the chart. "She needs to talk with our chief surgeon, Dr. Sterling. His office is on the fourth floor. Let me call and tell him you're on your way up." She picked up the phone and dialed a number. After a few minutes she looked at us and said, " He's up there now and will see you."

We got on the elevator and headed up to the fourth floor. "Gabriella, he's going to be all right."

"I'm sure of it, Cheryl. I knew it last night when I saw him. I could feel it, but I can't explain it."

We got off on the fourth floor and went straight to the doctor's office. His secretary showed me in and he introduced himself. "Hello, I'm Dr. Sterling. You must be Miss Newman. I'm the one who performed the surgery on Mr. Cannon."

"I'm glad to meet you, Dr. Sterling. I only wish it were under different circumstances. I hope you have good news for me about Jack."

"We still have a long way to go yet, but making it through the surgery last night is very positive. I don't want you to get your hopes up too high because there is much more that still has to happen before I feel he will be safe. I do hope that you don't mind me being so frank about his condition, but that's the way I am with all my patients and their relatives. I don't like surprises creeping up later."

He looked at me for approval, and I instantly liked this man. Dr. Sterling looked to be in his early fifties, and had a head full of hair that looked like he never combed it. Other than that, he looked like the typical doctor who was a little pale from not being out in the sun. Very clean and neat, down to the fingernails. I knew this man wouldn't pull any punches, and I liked that. "I'm glad that's the way you feel. Jack would want it that way, and I'm here for whatever Jack needs. Can you tell me more about what happens next?"

"Miss Newman, he's still in very critical condition. Right now it's still 50-50, and way too early to tell just which way it will go. Jack lost a lot of blood. Most of it was through internal bleeding. The bullets shattered when they entered his body. They were intended to kill him and almost did. Last night we got out as much as we dared of the fragments. He was getting very weak so we stopped. Now we'll wait twenty-four to forty-eight hours, monitor his condition before going back in again, and see what we have left. We can't wait any longer than that. Either way, we go back in by Monday morning. Don't expect too much from him in the next few days because he probably won't wake up at all. He's still very weak. Now, do you have any questions for me?" he asked as if he were just taking a deep breath before he would continue.

"I only have one question or request. Make that two. Please keep me informed of his condition, and I would like to stay in the room with him if that could be arranged."

"No problem with the first one Miss Newman, but I will have to insist that until we have him more stable that you stay only for short periods of time. We can't afford any chances of infection from outside sources. As soon as we get him stable, we'll fix you right up. This guy gets top priority around here, and that comes from the top. I don't know who he is, but somebody's got a lot of pull for him."

"Dr. Sterling, how long and how often can I see him then? I want to be near in case he does wake up, and please, call me Gabriella".

"Let's start with about fifteen minutes at a time and just watch his condition. I would only say about every other hour or so shouldn't be a problem. I would suggest that after you see him this morning that you go get some rest. He is still very heavily sedated, and I'm sure he won't even know you're around. Of course, that's entirely your decision," he said, rather apologetically.

"Just one more thing, Dr. Sterling. He *is* going to be all right. There is no doubt about it."

"We hope so, Gabriella. I'm always impressed by people with good attitudes."

"So is Jack. I want to see him now, if it's all right with you."

"By all means. I need to make my rounds anyway. I'll talk with you later."

I rose from my chair, shook his hand, and left his office in almost a run to see Jack. Cheryl was waiting outside and we went straight to the room.

"Gabriella, is everything all right?" she asked.

"It will be, but it might take a while. I can only see him for fifteen minutes right now and that bothers me. Other than that, he has more surgery to go through, and I'm scared to death." I began to cry again.

"Now, you can't let him see you like that. Let's stop at the restoom for a minute and fix you up again. OK?"

"OK," was all I could say at that moment.

Jack looked exactly the same as he did when I saw him last night. I was sure he hadn't moved an inch. I reached out and placed my hand on his and held it tightly. Then I leaned down and kissed him very gently on the lips. They were warm, but the feeling was lost somewhere in his body. Finally, I whispered, "Jack, I'm here just like I said I would be. I love you. Please hurry up and get better." I spent the rest of the time sitting on the bed holding his hand. The nurse came too quickly, though, and told me to leave. I could have hated her for that, but I knew she was just doing her job. I leaned down and kissed Jack again. "I'll be back soon. Don't leave without me."

As we were leaving, Cheryl asked, "When can you see him again?"

"In a couple of hours."

"Why don't we get a bite to eat, get you a shower, and we can be back by 1:30."

"What time is it anyway?"

"About noon."

"No wonder I was getting hungry. Is there a restaurant in the hotel where you guys have me staying?"

"Sure is, and the restaurant is usually not very busy and we won't have trouble getting in and out. The food's pretty good, too."

7

I ORDERED MY FOOD AND WAS DONE EATING before Cheryl had a chance to get started. I didn't mean to eat so fast, because we had plenty of time. It was a combination of being very hungry and wanting to get back to the hospital. I sat there quietly as Cheryl finished her lunch. I knew she was hurrying, but she had a pained look on her face. "Cheryl, slow down. We have plenty of time. I just got carried away."

"I thought you were in a hurry," she said as she gulped down the last of her food.

"I'm sorry, I should have said something sooner."

"Never mind, it'll find it's way to my stomach soon enough. Let's get you up to your room," she laughed.

I was surprised to find that the FBI does a really good job when it comes to making accommodations for people. They had an entire suite for me at the Sheraton, with more room than I would need. It had a separate bedroom with a king-size bed, and bath that was huge. The other room had a large dining area with a refrigerator, plus a separate living room with a large color TV. It even had a desk with all the supplies for an office. All I wanted was a place to take a shower and sleep for a few hours. It's such a shame that Jack and I couldn't share this together. I just knew that as soon as he's well, we'd make the best of it.

I opened one of the walk-in closets and all of Jack's clothes were neatly hung up in their proper places or folded neatly on the shelf. Next, I went to the other closet and they had done the same with mine. I walked to the dresser and everything was in place there too. It must have been a woman who put the things away. No man would have taken so much time. "Cheryl, they sure got our things here in a hurry."

"We didn't want to take any chances of leaving anything around. It only took me about an hour to unpack it after they got it here."

"I knew it had to be a woman. Thanks. When did you do it?"

"About six this morning. They called me last night and I was here at five. Just part of the job. Don't worry, I've done it many times before."

I grabbed a few things from the appropriate place in the closet and dresser and headed to the shower. "I'll only be a few minutes, but if you would like to lie down, I'll wake you when I'm ready."

"Thanks, Gabriella, but I'm fine. Besides, I have to guard you all the time."

"OK, I'll be ready in about fifteen minutes."

I stood under the shower and just let the water run over me for as long as I dared. I began to think of the time that Jack and I had taken our first shower together. We showered together until the water got cold, and almost froze before tore ourselves from the stall. Then I remembered the time we found each other again and that first night. I took a quick shower that night in Colorado and came out of the shower with a towel wrapped around me. Jack made such a big deal about it. He talked for days about how beautiful he thought I was. This guy is really crazy about me and also blind. Of course, I would never tell him that. I love the way he makes me feel beautiful.

I came back to reality quickly, finished showering, and was ready within a half-hour. We headed out of the room and I saw that Cheryl was looking very tired. "Are you all right?"

"I only get tired when I'm not busy, but don't worry. In our business there's a lot of waiting around. You sure get ready in a hurry. Missing Jack, are you?"

"Desperately. I only wish I could hold him in my arms and feel the same response from him. Remind me to tell you about the times I actually wouldn't let him even hold my hand."

"I can tell you really love him now, and that's what's important."

"I loved him then, too, but that's a long story and I'll tell you about that later."

When we arrived back at the hospital, I went straight to the nurses' station. "Can I see Jack now?"

"Miss Newman, you'll have to wait about another hour. Just have a seat in the waiting room," the nurse said.

"Has there been any change in his condition or has he awakened at all?"

"None," she said. "I'll call you when you can see him."

Cheryl and I again went to the waiting room. I just knew that I was going to end up hating this room. I grabbed a magazine and sat down just about the same place I was before. There weren't many people in now although the place had been packed in the morning. As I began to look through a current issue of *People* magazine, I noticed that this very tall, slender black man was staring at me. Not in a bad way, but more in a curious way. When he saw me looking, he turned away and looked out the window. He had a light complexion and I noticed he had a rather long, braided strand of hair hanging down his back. He didn't seem like anyone I needed to worry about, and Cheryl didn't seem to notice him. He was dressed like he might be going out to play basketball. He was wearing Reebok high-top tennis shoes, shorts, and an Orlando Magic jersey with the number 32 on it.

I continued to look at the magazine. Someone standing directly in front of me startled me. I looked up and the guy was there. He looked to be about seven-feet tall and I had to lean back to see his face.

"You must be Gabriella. Steve said you would be here. He described you pretty close. Am I right?"

"Yes, I'm Miss Newman. Who are you?" I asked rather harshly. Who was this guy anyway? Some agent or something?

"I'm sorry. I'm Gary Stephens. An old friend of Jack's. I hope he told you about me."

Somehow Jack had done it to me again. When he was talking about Gary the other day, he never described him to me, and I had a totally different image of him. He loves to have people make images of other people and finds out they are wrong. Anyway, Gary must have been a good guy or Jack wouldn't have requested that he work with us.

"Gary, it's really nice to meet you. And, yes, Jack did tell me about you. I just never expected you to be dressed to play basketball."

"Gabriella, in my world, this is dressed up. Only kidding," a big smile came over his face.

It was warm and drew you inside this person. He had kind eyes, and seemed to be what I needed. Someone who knew enough about Jack to help me understand. The other detail that I noticed about Gary was a neatly trimmed goatee. Oh yes, and he was always talking with his hands and moving around. Not like he was nervous, it was just his way of expressing himself.

"How long have you been here, Gary?"

"I got here about an hour ago. They said you just left. I decided to just wait here for you. How is Jack doing? I couldn't believe what had happened when Steve told me."

I filled him in with what information I had.

"Don't worry, Gabriella. Jack will be all right. I never met a more positive person in my life. This guy can beat any odds on his attitude alone."

"I see he worked on you, too," and we began to laugh.

"I'm Cheryl Hunter, Gary. Nice to meet you," she said as she extended her hand.

"I'm sorry, Cheryl. I didn't mean to leave you out," I replied.

"Nice to meet you, Cheryl. Steve told me about you two, and you're both as attractive as he said you would be."

"He has a tendency to exaggerate at times, I'm afraid," Cheryl said.

"Not this time." He reached out with both hands and shook hers ever so easily. This guy knew how to impress a woman.

"When do you get to see Jack again?" Gary asked.

"Soon, I hope. The nurse said she would come and get me in a little while. I know that if she doesn't come in the next few minutes, I'll go hunt down Dr. Sterling. I'm in no mood to play games," I said boldly.

"She'll be here soon, Gabriella," Cheryl said.

"Yeah, they won't make you wait any longer than necessary. Besides that, they don't want the 'man' on them," Gary gestured to himself with his hands, moving half his body at the same time.

"You have a way with words, Gary," I said.

"When you're as tall as I am, people tend to listen."

"How tall are you, anyway?" Cheryl asked.

"About 6'5"."

"I'm glad you're on our team."

"I'm just a puppy dog. Don't let the size fool you."

The nurse entered the room and interrupted. "Miss Newman, you can see Jack now."

"Thank you. You guys will just have to excuse me. I need to see Jack."

"We'll be all right, you just go," Cheryl said.

I walked in the room and Jack was lying just the way I had left him earlier. There did seem to be more color in his face, but everything else was the same. I sat down on the bed next to him, and leaned over and kissed him on the cheek before I said, "I love you, Jack. I'm here with you now. Did you miss me?" I guess I expected him to open his eyes and say, "Very much," but I got no response. I knew that he heard me, and he understood. I took a brush from my purse and ran it through the little bit of hair that he had. I remembered all the kidding he had taken from his students about his balding. I never once saw him get upset about it. In fact, he used to thrive on that kind of stuff. "Don't look at what's on my head. Look at what's in my heart. A hairy heart." They would all laugh. Anyway, I combed what little he had.

As I was sitting there, a buzzer started going off. Then another, and another. *What is going on?* I thought. This can't be normal. A nurse came running in.

"Miss Newman, you'll have to leave," she said as she pushed me aside. "His blood pressure is dropping," she said to the other nurse as she entered the room.

"Should I get the doctor?" the second nurse asked.

"Yes."

I looked at the name tag on the nurse's uniform and saw the name Stovall. "Miss Stovall, what's wrong?"

"Miss Newman, I told you that you must leave. Now."

As I was leaving I heard one of them say, "We'll have to go back in now. He's losing too much blood." I almost fainted there on the spot.

The next thing I knew, they were wheeling him down the hall toward surgery. There must have been six people around his bed. There were all types of equipment around him as they traveled down the hall.

As Dr. Sterling passed, he stopped only to say, "We have to operate again. I'll let you know what's going on as soon as possible," and he was gone.

I began to cry. I felt these hands on my shoulders and turned around to see Gary there. I put my arms around his waist, buried my head in his chest, and cried out of control.

"Gabriella, he's going to be all right," I heard Cheryl saying.

"Yeah, remember what I told you. This guy will make it on attitude alone," Gary said.

"I just don't want to lose him. I love him so very much."

"I don't want to hear anymore talk like that. He's going to be fine and don't you forget it," Gary said.

"Gary, you sound just like him," I said through the tears.

"He works on everybody, doesn't he?"

"I have to get to know Jack as soon as he gets better. Sounds like a great guy," Cheryl said.

"He is," Gary said.

We went back to the waiting room and did just that. Waited. It was about 2:00 P.M. I hoped that he would be out of surgery soon.

8

*J*ACK WAS STILL IN SURGERY hours later. No one had any answers. All I could find out was that he was still in the operating room and I was smart enough to figure that out. I tried not to think like that, but the pressure was getting to me. He had to be all right.

At 7:30 Dr. Sterling came into the waiting room. He looked totally exhausted. He wiped the sweat from his forehead as he walked up. "He's OK for now, Gabriella. We almost lost him a couple of times. Those fragments are all over his insides, and I'm still not sure we got them all. We did stop the bleeding again, and his vital signs are stable. I've got to warn you, though. He is very weak and his chances have gone down some. The surgery was almost too much on him. But he's a strong guy and holding on. We'll know more by morning and I'm afraid that it will be morning before you can see him."

I felt Cheryl's arm around my waist. I started to cry again. I had always considered myself a strong person, but this was just too much.

"Dr. Sterling, could I just sit in the room with him? I promise I won't get in the way. He might wake up and I just want to be with him," I begged through my tears.

"Let me see what I can arrange with the nurses, Gabriella. I can't promise you anything, though. We usually don't make exceptions for anyone. I'll be back in a few minutes," and he was gone.

"I told you he'd make it," I heard Gary saying.

"This is almost too much to bear. I have to be with him."

"Leave it to Dr. Sterling. He'll work something out. He's the boss around here," Cheryl said.

"I sure hope so."

After a few minutes, Dr. Sterling returned and said, "I talked with Mrs. Stovall. She said she would try to work something out. She asked that you be patient and she would be out to talk to you as soon as she got Jack settled in intensive care. I have to go now, but I'll be where they can get me if I'm needed."

"Thank you, Dr. Sterling. I realize you're tired. Thank you."

"I guess he does have a lot of pull around here," Gary said, as the doctor walked off.

We sat back down in the waiting room. Cheryl said, "He's been the chief of surgery here for more than ten years and is very well respected. You couldn't have a better doctor for Jack than Dr. Sterling."

"I'm glad he's here. He doesn't pull any punches, and I know I'm hearing the whole truth when I talk with him. I wish the nurse would hurry up."

Just give them some time, Gabriella. I'm sure they want Jack to be taken care of first," Gary said.

"Gabriella, why don't we run down to the café downstairs and get a quick bite to eat. We'll tell the nurse where to find us," Cheryl suggested.

I *was* hungry, but I was more interested in seeing Jack first. I know it's probably hard for them to understand about Jack and I, but they will just have to accept it for now. Gary sensed my hesitation.

"Let's wait a few more minutes, and see if Mrs. Stovall gets here. I'd hate to just sit down and then not get to eat," Gary said.

"That's what I prefer, Cheryl. I hope you understand."

"That's fine, Gabriella. I just thought it would help the time go by quicker."

"Let's just wait a while longer."

The nurse came in the room about fifteen minutes later, and sat down beside me. "Miss Newman, Jack is set up in intensive care and very heavily sedated. Before I take you down to see him, I want to explain what will happen for the next twenty-four hours. He is set up in an oxygen tent, and we are going to be watching him very closely. There will be nurses in his room at all times to do different tests. I'll let you sit with him about ten minutes every hour."

"I appreciate even that amount of time, Mrs. Stovall. I promise I won't get in the way."

"I have to warn you that he looks different since the long surgery. He is a lot paler, but don't worry. He's holding his own now."

"Is there anything else I should know, Mrs. Stovall?"

"Yes, my first name is Jo," and she began to smile.

That was the first time I realized that she could smile. Before that, it had been all business. "Thank you, Jo. Please call me Gabriella."

"Are you ready to see him?"

"Ready," I said. We got up and left the room.

The room that I entered this time looked more like a lab than a room someone would be in when they are sick. Jack was in the middle of the room with all kinds of machines attached to him. When I looked at him, I almost fainted. His face was all drawn up, and his eyes were set deep in his head. He was very pale, and looked to be very far away. I tried my best to keep the tears from coming, but it was no use. I turned and went to the corner of the room, and sat down until I could regain control. How could all of this be happening to us after what we had already been through? Then I remembered that Jack was still alive and he would be all right. I walked back over to the bed, and looked down at Jack through the oxygen tent. I took his hand and held it tightly. "Jack, I'm here with you. Everything is going to be fine. I'll be here when you wake up. Please remember that I love you." I stood by the bed until the nurse asked that I leave so they could do some tests.

Gary and Cheryl were talking in the waiting room when I returned. "Are you guys ready to eat yet? I'm starving." They both looked up at me and seemed startled.

"How is Jack?" Gary asked.

"He's going to be fine. He doesn't look much like himself right now, but I'm positive he will be OK."

"Then let's go get something to eat," Cheryl said.

We took the elevator down to the cafeteria. We must have all been hungry, because each one of us went back through the line a second time. It was now getting very late, and I wanted to find out what the plan would be for the rest of the night. "Cheryl, are you going home tonight, and then coming back in the morning?"

"Until we are sure that everything is safe again, I'm assigned to you twenty-four hours a day. I have some clothes in the other room in your suite."

I hadn't even noticed that there was another room. "So that means whatever I do, you have to do, too?"

"Pretty much."

"I hope you don't mind, but I plan on spending the night here at the hospital. I just want to make sure I'm around if he needs me."

"That's OK. I'll just get some sleep in the waiting room. Maybe in the morning we could go to the room so I could take a shower?"

"I'll have to have one, too, or Jack might not want me to be around," I joked.

"What are you going to do, Gary? I mean, what plans do you have now that you're here?"

"I'm here to stay now. The reason I'm here at all is that Jack wanted my help. I have a room in the hotel where you're at, and I'm just going to hang until we can get started on the program."

"That's great, Gary. I'm going to need all the reassurance I can get until Jack gets better."

"I think I'll go to the room in a little while and get some sleep, then come back later. Will you guys be all right 'til I get back?"

"Gary, you have to remember that Cheryl isn't just a pretty face. She's here to protect me."

"I'm sorry, Cheryl. I just said that as a general statement. I'm sure you're very good at what you do. Besides that, your beauty made me lose my train of thought," he said and started to laugh.

"OK, Gary, you're starting to sound like Jack now. You must have hung around him too long."

"I guess I'll just have to body slam him before he realizes that I'm really an agent," Cheryl said.

We finished eating dinner and went back to the waiting room. Gary stayed for a few minutes and then left for the hotel. Cheryl grabbed a couple of books, pulled off her shoes, and began to read. I just sat waiting for the nurse to come and tell me that it was all right to see Jack again. My mind began to wander through all the events that had occurred that day and I became very tired. Just as I was about to doze off, a nurse came in and tapped me on the shoulder.

"Miss Newman, you can come in the room now."

"Are there any changes in his condition?"

"None at all, and at this point, that's what we want."

During the rest of the night, everything was quiet. Jack didn't seem to move at all. He was still a very sick man and they assured me that everything was normal for someone that had this type of surgery. He still looked so very weak. I missed hearing his voice.

9

*F*OUR DAYS PASSED AND THERE WAS STILL NO CHANGE in Jack's condition. I had been at the hospital the whole time, except to take a shower and change clothes. Cheryl and I were becoming very close. She stayed by my side the whole time. Gary was there also. He only left for short periods of time with Steve to work on the case. Oh yes, Steve. He was there too. We were all just waiting, and I was going crazy. Dr. Sterling assured me that everything was as good as it could be at this point. His condition wasn't better, but it wasn't worse either. He said that Jack could stay this way for an indefinite time, but that is still better than the alternative. There was no internal bleeding and his condition was still stable.

"Jack, I'm still here with you. I still love you and I want you to hurry up and get better," I whispered to him when no one was in the room. It was now into the fifth day and there was still no change. I had already showered and changed clothes for the day. It was my third visit of the day and this was all becoming a normal pattern for us. Cheryl and Gary were down in the waiting room and they had brought along cards to help pass time. "I'll be back later, Jack," I said to him as I was leaving the room. I made my way back to the waiting room and took up my usual position in there.

"Any change?" Cheryl asked as she looked up from their game of rummy.

"None at all. I'm getting worried that he may stay that way forever."

"Gabriella, I don't want to hear that kind of talk," Gary said.

"It's been five days already. What am I supposed to think?"

"You're supposed to give it time, just like the doctor said," Gary continued.

"That's easy for you to say. You're not the one who needs him," I said in a harsh voice. It was too late to change what I had said. Open mouth, insert foot. I sure did it this time.

"I'll be back later," Gary said as he got up.

"Gary, I'm sorry. You know I didn't mean it that way," I said as I got up and went over to him. "Please forgive me."

"I can see how Jack got hooked up with you. That look you have on your face could win an award. Look, I know you're getting frustrated, but he's going to be all right. OK?"

"I know Gary. I'm sorry."

"Quit looking at me like that. I forgive you."

I put my arms around him and held him tightly. I needed him here with me and it sure was a relief that he was. "Gary, I'm the one who's lucky. To love Jack and have a friend like you. And, of course, you too, Cheryl."

"You'd better include me," she said laughing.

"Miss Newman, we need you in Mr. Cannon's room if you have a minute," the nurse said.

"What's wrong?" I said, almost afraid to ask. It wasn't time for me to be in the room. There must be something wrong.

"Just come with me, please," she ordered.

We entered the room where Jack was and Mrs. Stovall was there. "Gabriella, just have a seat for a minute," she said.

"Jo, what's wrong? Is Jack all right?"

"Just a minute, Gabriella."

I couldn't see anything any different in the room, but there was a lot more activity. Usually there was only one nurse in there, but now there were three. What could be going wrong?

"Gabriella, come over here. Could you keep an eye on Jack for a minute? I'll be right back."

"Jo, what's the matter? Is Jack all right?"

"I'm sorry I startled you. Nothing's wrong. We just had to change our schedule. I hope you don't mind."

"No, it's OK. I was worried that something might be wrong with Jack."

"You've got ten minutes from now," she said smiling and left the room.

I turned around and looked down at Jack. As usual, I reached down and held his hand. "Jack, I'm back a little early, but I'm back just like I promised. I love you." As I said the words, I felt pressure on my hand. I thought I must have been imagining it because of all the time I'd been there, but then I felt the pressure again. "Jack, if you hear me, squeeze my hand again." There was pressure again. I looked around for a nurse to tell. I looked for the buttons so I could call one of the nurses. I looked down at Jack. There was no change in his face at all. I had to get a nurse. I started to pull my hand out of Jack's hand. I looked down at Jack and said, "Hold on, I'll be right back."

In the quietest of voices I had ever heard, the words came out, "Gabriella, I love you."

I could barely hear the words, but they were his. I began to cry. Jack was going to be all right. I looked down at him again and he opened his eyes very slowly.

He did his best to smile at me, and I could tell he was still very weak. "Please don't say another word. Just kiss me so I know that you're really here," he said in an almost inaudible voice.

I leaned down and gently kissed him on the lips, and then on the cheek. I whispered to him, "I told you that I would never leave you again and I never will. We're going to be together forever. Now that you know I'm here, get some rest and we'll talk later." As I rose from the bed, I noticed the nurse coming. I was still crying and couldn't stop. What a relief it was to finally hear his voice.

"Gabriella, don't be mad at the nurses. I made them do it," he said, closing his eyes. There was a smile on his face as he went back to sleep.

"Jo, what was Jack talking about?"

"Well, just as you were leaving the last time, he began to wake up. The first word out of his mouth was your name. I told him that I would get you. He was conscious enough to tell me not to tell you he was awake yet. He made me promise. Then he asked that I go get you and he would handle the rest. That's quite a guy you have there," she said.

With tears still running down my eyes I said, "I'm going to kick his butt when he's well enough."

I ran down to the waiting room to tell Cheryl and Gary the good news. I entered the door and they both hurried to greet me.

"He's conscious, isn't he?" Gary shouted.

"Yes," I said and threw my arms around him.

"Gabriella, I'm so very happy for you. What great news," Cheryl continued. Then she joined in our embraces. The three of us were holding each other. Cheryl and I were crying and Gary was doing his best not to.

"I think it's time for a celebration, and I've been ready since I got here. Anybody want to join me? I say we do it tonight," Gary said.

"I agree, Gary, and tonight sounds great. What about you, Cheryl?"

"I hate to say this, but I'll have to check with Steve first. We might have to confine our celebration to the room at the hotel," she said, putting on her agent's hat again.

"We are going to party somewhere tonight, Cheryl. With or without Steve's approval. You understand?" Gary said.

"I understand."

We all began to laugh and cry at the same time. It was time for some sort of celebration. I knew it might be a little premature, but just to hear his voice and see his eyes open was all I needed to make my whole body come alive again. I need to talk with Dr. Sterling. He will give me the answer I need. I hope.

"Jo, has Dr. Sterling looked at Jack yet?" I said as I entered the room for my next visit.

"Not yet. He was in surgery all morning, and should be here in the next hour. We did send word to him through one of the nurses. I'm sure he'll be here as soon as he gets a chance."

"Has Jack been awake since the last time I was here?"

"No. He'll probably sleep the rest of the day. He's still very weak. He might wake again when Dr. Sterling examines him. Then again, he may sleep through the whole thing. We'll just have to wait and see."

"Do you think Dr. Sterling will let me stay in here during the examination."

"We might be able to convince him," she said as she winked at me and smiled.

The rest of my time with him, I just sat there holding his hand and staring at him. I imagined him smiling, but he looked more at peace than he did before. I ran my finger through what little hair he had and again thought of all the jokes we always made about his hair. What an easygoing guy. He would do anything for anyone he cared at all about. Dr. Sterling still hadn't arrived by the time I had to leave. I made my way back to the waiting room to wait again.

Dr. Sterling walked in the waiting room about thirty minutes later. He sat down beside me and began by saying, "I see your boyfriend has decided to join us again. It's about time he started getting with the program, wouldn't you say?"

"I'm so happy that I couldn't begin to tell you in words. Have you examined him yet, Dr. Sterling?"

"Not yet. I wanted to talk with you first. I want you to understand what we might be up against. I think from what I have heard, that his mind and voice are in good shape, but I want to examine him completely. I understand that you want to be there. May I suggest that you let me do a preliminary examination and then I will send for you. That way I may be able to tell you more. Is that OK with you, Gabriella?"

I felt like screaming, "No, it's not. I want to be there." Instead I just said, "If you think that's the best for Jack. Please let me know as soon as possible what his condition is."

"I'll send a nurse for you in just a little while. Thanks for being so understanding," he said as he got up to leave.

"Everything's going to be all right, Gabriella," Cheryl said.

"You've got to give the man time to do his job. He wants to make sure all the fingers and toes are working," Gary said, smiling.

"Thanks guys, but I just want to be there. I want to see what's going on, and I want to be able to talk with him. I know you both understand how I feel."

When I was finally able to go back to his room, I saw that Jack was unconscious and Dr. Sterling was leaning over him listening to his heart. He signaled me to come over to the bed.

"Gabriella, watch this." Dr. Sterling began pricking him with a needle to get some response from the body. "Please notice that from the waist down there is no response. There does seem to be some response in the hands and arms. I don't mean to alarm you with all this, but you wanted to know what was going on. It's still very early."

"Thank you, Dr. Sterling."

"The best thing we can do now is let him rest and build up his strength. I'll examine him again in the morning. Jo, page me if he regains consciousness," Dr. Sterling said. "I have patients to see now."

"Thanks again, Dr. Sterling," I said as he left the room.

"Gabriella, we need to let him rest now. You can come back in an hour or so," Jo said.

I leaned down, kissed him softly on the cheek, and said, "I love you, Jack. I'll be back in an hour." Again I made my way back to the waiting room.

"Well, Gabriella, do we celebrate or not?" Gary said.

"I think we need to celebrate regardless. It wasn't totally what I wanted to hear, but he is going to recover and that alone is worth a celebration. Cheryl, did you check with Steve and get his OK?"

"He said he thought that it would be all right as long as we didn't draw too much attention to ourselves. Gary, that means you have to behave."

"Do you know what you're asking?"

"It's either that or we go play basketball," she said laughing and pretending to make a shot at an imaginary hoop.

"OK, I'll behave. You know I'm too short for B-ball. Gabriella, what time does this grand event occur, and where?"

"It will have to be near the hospital, and they'll have to know where I am in case Jack needs me. Any ideas?" I asked them both.

"Cheryl, this is your hometown. Gabriella and I are both newcomers. You pick the place. It has to be someplace we can dance, though," Gary said as he started moving parts of his body I didn't know moved. Cheryl and I both laughed and just shrugged our shoulders.

"There is a place a couple of blocks down from the hotel that we could go. I think they play top forties stuff, but I'm not sure."

"As long as it's not country. I don't have anything against that kind of music, but I like more contemporary music when I go out. You know what I mean? A beat I can dance to like 'Freaky With You'."

"Hey, I can tell everything will be fine. What kind of music do you like to dance to Cheryl?" Gary said.

"I only like to slow dance. I never ever fast dance."

"We'll see."

"I'm serious, Gary."

"So am I."

"What time is it anyway?" I asked.

"It's 5:30 now. What time do you want to leave here?" Cheryl asked.

"Let's stay until about 8:00 so that I can see Jack a couple of more times. If he's OK, then we'll leave. That sound all right with you guys?"

"Great," Gary said.

"Me, too," Cheryl agreed.

10

*I*T WAS ABOUT 8:15 WHEN I LEFT JACK'S ROOM to go take a shower, eat, and celebrate his recovery. He hadn't regained consciousness since earlier in the day, but the nurse assured me that it was normal. I made sure the hospital knew where and how to reach me, and told them I'd call later to check in. I just wish Jack were going with me. I wanted to hold him. But instead, we were celebrating his being alive and recovering. It was very close to being completely over. I thanked God for giving us another chance. I'm sure he had something in store for us.

We arrived at the lounge about 10:30. It was a rather small place with a small dance floor, which was already full. There was a DJ who seemed to know what he was doing, and playing some pretty good music. The place was dimly lit, and had only a few tables. The minute we walked in, Gary was already moving all those parts of his body and more. The guy could dance. He walked up to an attractive blonde, asked her to dance, and was on his way.

"Cheryl, I guess we better order a drink for ourselves if we want one. It looks as though Gary may be gone for a while."

"I think you're right. What kind do you want, and I'll go get it," Cheryl volunteered.

"I think I'll have a White Russian. That's Jack's favorite drink and this is for him. What do you drink?"

"I like margarita's without the salt. I acquired a taste for those while I was in college. I can't drink many, though," she said. "I'll be right back."

I suddenly felt very lonely. I missed Jack. I felt guilty being here, but I knew there was nothing I could do at the hospital. If Jack were awake, he would have insisted that I go. He knew that my every being belongs to him and wouldn't worry. I decided to call the hospital and went to the bar to explain my situation to the bartender who gave me the number for the phone behind the bar to pass on to the hospital. The bartender, Sue, said just to have them call it and she would make sure I got the message. I tried to give her a big tip as Cheryl was paying for our drinks, but she wouldn't take it. With that taken care of, I felt better.

Cheryl and I made our way as near to the dance floor as we could get. Gary was taller than anyone on the floor, and was easy to spot. He looked over at us and smiled like a little kid who had just got out for recess. He was having a ball. This was his environment. When the song ended, he came over to us, still dancing.

"Where's my drink?"

"Now how were we supposed to know what you wanted to drink? Much less if we would ever see you again," Cheryl said.

"I just liked the song that was playing and when I get started, it's hard to stop. Anyway, let me grab me a drink and I'll be back. Then the real dancing begins. Who's first?"

"It has to be Gabriella unless it's a slow song. I don't fast dance."

"I better get you another drink, because we are going to dance to whatever is playing."

"Get her a margarita with no salt, and I'll have a White Russian since you're buying," I said laughing.

"You guys don't go away," he told us

"Where would we go anyway?" Cheryl said.

When Gary got back with our drinks, we all looked at each other, and knew what had to be the next move. "I would like to make a toast to one of the greatest guys I know. To a great friend and to the reason we are all here tonight. To Jack," Gary said.

"To the man I love and to his quick recovery."

"To success in our future endeavors," Cheryl added.

We downed our drinks quickly, and Gary grabbed my hand and pulled me out to the dance floor. "Don't move Cheryl. I'll be back for you after two songs. Do you understand?"

"You'll never find me."

Gary took me to the far side of the dance floor so that Cheryl could hardly see us. "I'm going to dance one song with you, then I'd like for you to stay over on this side of the dance floor. I'm going to sneak over and get Cheryl before she has a chance to hide."

"That sounds just like something that Jack would do. How long did you know him before you guys split up?"

"Almost two years. He actually saved my life, and I owe him a lot. That's why when they called and asked me to come, I would never have refused. I thought I would never hear from him again." We danced in silence until the song ended. "OK, Gabriella, just hide and watch this."

He made his way around the dance floor so fast that I had a hard time keeping up with him. The next thing I knew, I saw him with Cheryl on the dance floor. I have no idea how he made her dance, but he looked over and winked at me.

At that very moment, my thoughts went back to Jack. I wished he could be there with me. I couldn't wait until he was one hundred percent again so that we can do all the things that we use to do. I wanted to leave that very minute to be by his side. But Cheryl and Gary had been so understanding and needed a little time for some fun. I could stay a little longer.

They danced together for a long time. The funny thing was that every song was a fast one. As Jack had said to me, what seemed like a very long time ago, "Never say never. You'll end up having to eat your words."

About midnight they finally played a slow song. I thought they might come off the dance floor then, but they continued. After that song ended, they slowly walked over to where I was standing. They were both dripping with perspiration.

"Don't you dare say a word," Cheryl said smiling.

"I wasn't, except that to say you guys make a great looking couple out there."

"I think so, too," Gary said.

"I can't believe I let him get me out on the dance floor. I hope you know, we were keeping an eye on you. How many guys did you turn down anyway?" Cheryl asked.

"I didn't even count," I said and then I changed the subject. "Do you guys mind if we leave soon? I'd like to get back to the hospital to be with Jack."

"We were about ready to leave anyway. We could see the look in your eyes," Cheryl said.

"How about one dance with me before we leave?"

"Sure, Gary," I said, and we headed for the dance floor.

11

WE DROPPED GARY OFF AT THE HOTEL and went back to the hospital. I left Cheryl in the waiting room and went to be with Jack. He was lying there very quietly and looked content. Maybe even a little more rested than I had noticed before. I again leaned down and kissed him on the lips. As I touched his lips, I felt a response from him. Not very much, but enough that I could feel the response. As I kissed him again, he opened his eyes. I pulled back a little so that I could look into his eyes.

"I love you, Gabriella," he said very quietly.

"You know I love you, Jack. How are you feeling?"

"I feel very little because of all the drugs. The only real feeling I have right now is for you. Can you tell me what happened?"

"I better get a nurse right now. They told me to call them if there was any change. I'll explain everything else when you are stronger. OK?"

"Just don't go too far away."

"Impossible."

I looked down the hall and signaled one of the nurses to tell her that Jack had regained consciousness. She then went back to the nurses' station, and got on the phone for instructions. Soon after, two nurses came into the room followed by one of the doctors on call that night. When they had finished examining him, the doctor and one of the nurses left the room. The other nurse checked a few more things and then turned to me.

"We're finished for now, and he's asking for you."

"Thank you," I said as I returned my attention to Jack. I was a little surprised that he was still awake. "How are you feeling?"

"I'm not real sure. How about giving me a kiss so I can check to see how many of the parts are working," he asked with a small smile on his face.

I kissed him ever so softly on the lips, but with a little more passion. He responded more this time, and I could feel the life running from him to me and then returning to him. I wanted to be in his arms so desperately, but I was glad for what I was getting.

"I need to sleep now. Will you be here when I wake up again?"

"Jack, do you even have to ask?"

"Just kiss me one more time before I go to sleep. Please."

As 1 kissed him, he fell asleep again.

"Goodnight, my love."

12
Jack

I WAS STARTING TO GET MY STRENGTH BACK NOW. Gabriella had explained what happened and I felt lucky to be alive. I felt even luckier that I had Gabriella with me. If she had still been in Florida, I might not have the desire to live. It had been two days now since I had regained consciousness and I was able to stay awake for longer periods of time. That gave me more time to appreciate this woman that had ended up by my side. I can truly say that I must be the most blessed man alive. We were going to have a really great life together.

I had also learned from Dr. Sterling that my recovery might take quite a while. I had no feeling from my waist down, but he felt that it would come in time; I should recover completely.

During those same two days I had met Jo Stovall, the head nurse, and gave her a really hard time. I barely remember having her play my little trick on Gabriella, but it sure sounds like I had my mind working if nothing else. I also knew all the nurses by first name and flirted with all of them constantly. That is definitely a sign I was getting better. The only problem was that Gabriella had already warned them about me.

Today was the day that I was to meet Gary for the first time since eight yeas ago in Florida. They wouldn't let him visit until today, but Gabriella had told me how he was and he sounded just like the guy I'd become such close friends with when he wasn't even old enough to buy beer.

I would also get to meet with Steve and the agent that Gabriella had told me so much about. Cheryl Hunter sounded like a very efficient person and very attractive. I was anxious to find out how all of this was going to affect our plans for California. I guess it depended on my recovery, at least part of it. I was positive that Steve had already been working on it.

"Hi, beautiful lady, get over here and kiss me. I need that cure that comes from your kiss," I said as Gabriella entered the room. She walked over without saying a word and kissed me very passionately. What a woman! Every man should feel this sensation. The bottom half of me wasn't working, but my heart was.

"There are some people outside who have been waiting a long time to talk with you. Should I have them come in now?"

"Only after I hold you for a minute."

She walked over, put her arms around me, and kissed me again. "You're not getting tired of me yet, are you?" she whispered.

"Never," I replied. "Now you can have them come in."

Gary, Steve, and Cheryl came quietly into the room and were trying not to upset things. I had to do something to make them feel more comfortable.

"You guys aren't entering a funeral home. I'm very much alive and getting better everyday. So, with that in mind, lighten up. OK?"

Gary walked over to me and put out his hand, "How you feeling, Jack?"

"Come here, big guy," I said and I pulled him closer and hugged his neck. "I said I was better already. You don't have to be so careful. Gabriella's already been lying in bed with me."

"You look just like you did the last time I saw you, Jack. Well, maybe a little less hair."

"You'll pay for that when I can get out of this bed."

"You need to get better soon so I can win some of your money playing ball."

"No way, my man. I've gotten a lot smarter as I was getting older. I'm only going to play something I have a chance at. You control the basketball court. I'll find something I can give you a challenge at."

"You'd better get busy," he laughed.

"So, what do you think about our little plan?"

"We haven't really discussed it yet, Jack. We were going to wait and see how you were before we made any further plans. You've been a really sick guy," Steve said as he walked over and shook my hand.

"It's really good to see you again, Steve. I bet you were a little worried about the whole idea after I was shot."

"We won't have any more trouble with that, because we released that you had died from the gunshot wounds. It was in all the papers here in Denver."

"Do you think it worked?"

"I feel pretty sure it did. There are only a few people here who know who you really are, and what this is all about. It should work."

There was a very attractive blonde standing quietly in the corner. She seemed to be taking all this in and just waiting. She looked very professional, yet refreshingly beautiful.

"You must be Agent Hunter. I've heard a lot of good things about you from Gabriella."

"Please call me Cheryl. I'm glad you're OK. This is a great woman that's been here worrying about you," she said as she put her arm around Gabriella.

"She's as good as any man could ever want, and I'm extremely lucky to have her by my side. In fact, I'm a very lucky guy to have you all as friends."

"That's not going to work on us, Jack. We have a lot of work to do, and the vacation is over," Steve said laughing.

"Steve, Gabriella explained as much as she knew about Connie. Can you tell me just what's up? I'm sure she was very upset when she found out what had happened."

"Right about the time you were shot, she left on a school tour of Russia and has just arrived back. I called her and told her to fly to Denver and that you were seriously injured. She'll be here later this afternoon. I had an agent with her at the time and she's flying in with her. I'll bring her here as soon as she arrives."

"Why don't you let Gabriella go along since she knows Connie and can explain everything."

"I'd prefer that she not be seen with your daughter right now. We have to keep a very low profile."

"I understand. Connie's been around long enough that she will understand."

"She'll just be glad you're OK, Jack. I wish she had been here to help me cope with all of this. She's very strong," Gabriella said.

"Don't worry a bit, Jack. I'll get her here as quickly as I can," Steve said.

"Thanks, Steve. Now, next question. I know you've been planning, and I'm just curious what you have planned for us."

"Yeah, Steve. We're all a little curious now that we know Jack is going to be all right," Gary said.

"Well, since you asked and since I do have a plan, here goes. Now remember this is just a suggestion and subject to approval from all of you. First, we send Gary out to Virginia and start his training. Probably Monday. You and Gabriella stay here until you are ready to be moved. In the mean time, we'll send Cheryl out to California to start setting up things."

"You mean we get the great-looking blonde to work with us?" Gary said. "What a country."

"I haven't even talked it over with Cheryl yet, but if I know her, it won't be a problem," Steve continued, looking at her for approval.

"I was hoping that I might get to help in the case, especially since I know these guys so well now."

"Well, there you have it. After Gary finishes his training, he goes on out, and then you guys follow when you're ready. How's that sound, Jack?"

"That sounds fine with me, if it's all right with Gabriella. What do you think, honey?"

"I'll be ready when you are, sir," she said and saluted me.

"Real cute, ma'am," I said and we all laughed.

"OK, from here on, we start having regular meetings to set this up. These people are very clever and you guys will need all the training you have time for," Steve said.

"You have to remember that you are talking with the 'G-man' of the newly formed 'Posse,'" he said. "We'll make it work."

"Posse? Who came up with that?" I asked.

"Who do you think, man?"

"I should have known. Well, I guess we'll just have to keep it then. Got names for the rest of the Posse yet?"

"Not yet, but I'm working on it," Gary said as we laughed again.

"I can hardly wait to hear them," Gabriella said.

"You'd better be careful what you try to call me," Cheryl said.

"I'll make them good," Gary replied.

We spent the next couple of hours just talking about anything that came into our minds. For me, it was wonderful just to be able to listen. To think that six days ago I was as near death as anyone could be. I was happy just to be alive.

"Jack, Connie will be here soon and you look a little tired. Why don't you get some rest, and we'll come back when she gets here," Gabriella said.

"We sure don't want you to over do it. We have a job to do and you've been loafing long enough," Gary said.

"I am getting tired and I definitely don't want to fall asleep when Connie gets here. What time is it anyway?"

"It's 3:00," Cheryl said.

"We can talk again later," Steve added.

Gabriella leaned down, gave me a kiss, and whispered in my ear, "Please get some rest. I want you home soon. I have something to give you that will help you more than anything a doctor can give you."

I smiled up at her and said, "I have no doubt about that. I can hardly wait. I love you."

"I love you, too, Jack. Now close your eyes and get some rest."

"Just don't stay gone too long. Later everyone," I said as they were walking out the door.

I slept until about 8:00 P.M., when I was awakened by some people whispering in the corner of the room.

"He's going to be fine, Connie. The worst time was the first couple of nights when they were doing all the surgery. I was so scared," Gabriella whispered.

"I wish I could have been here with you. It must have been extremely tough on you," Connie said quietly.

"At least I had some special people here with me. Gary and Cheryl were my rock."

"Can I join in on the conversation, or is this a conversation for visitors only?" I asked and smiled at them.

Connie quickly came over to me, hugged me, and gave me a kiss. "Daddy, I'm sorry I wasn't here. I had just left for the trip to Russia. I love you. Are you feeling better?"

"Slow down, sweetheart. Everything is all right. You don't need to be sorry about anything. How was your trip?"

"It was great, but let's talk about you. Are you sure you're all right? Is there anything I can get you?"

"I'm fine. I'm very weak, and it will just be a matter of time before I'm ready to go. I hope you didn't worry too much when they told you what had happened."

"Just don't do this again. I'm sure Gabriella and I would have to kick your butt."

"To tell you the truth, I hope it never happens again to me or anyone else."

"And you guys are putting yourself right back in the same kind of risk. Are you crazy, Daddy?"

"You know why we're doing it. Besides, this is different. We're going to get some training before we start."

"I know, Daddy, but it will still be dangerous."

"Connie, we're just going to do this one thing, one time, and that's all. Gabriella and I feel it's just too much to pass up. There are just too many people that are being affected by these drugs. Please try and understand."

"What's really wrong, is that I do understand and envy you. I love you, Daddy, and I love Gabriella, and I think you guys are wonderful. I wish I could help."

"Forget it. I don't want to have to worry about you too. We'll get this done. You just get your fanny back to school and take care of your education. Do you understand, young lady?"

"If you weren't my dad, I'd tell you what to do with your 'young lady' crap. But, no problem. You guys can handle it."

With all the excitement, I almost forgot how tired I was. I was getting very weak and could hardly hold my eyes open. They were all talking and having such a good time. These were my kind of people. Full of life.

* * *

"Good morning, darling," I heard Gabriella saying. "Did you sleep well?"

"What happened? The last thing I remember was listening to you guys talking about something. I can't remember what."

"You fell asleep. You were saying how good it was to have us all together and you just closed your eyes and fell asleep. Did you sleep well?"

"I guess I did. I don't remember anything until I just heard your voice. Have I told you how beautiful you are lately?"

"It's about time. I was beginning to wonder if you still thought so, Jack. I'm kidding. I love you."

13

*T*HE NEXT WEEK GARY AND CHERYL LEFT FOR VIRGINIA to start an abbreviated training program. Steve had decided that they both should be sent in about the same time. He wanted them ready in about six weeks. Gary was pretty excited that Cheryl was going to be around for some additional training with him.

"Steve, you mean to tell me that I'm going to be forced to go through training with Cheryl! What kind of guy do you think I am anyway? She doesn't have a chance when it comes to training camp with me. I didn't know she even knew how to play basketball," Gary joked.

"What she'll be able to teach you will put you to shame. She was one of our top recruits and she's going to kick your butt," Steve replied.

"Just wait till I get hold of you. You may be good at basketball, but we'll see who gets the best shots," Cheryl said as we all laughed.

As for Connie, Gabriella, and me, we spent the next week pretty much like the others since the shooting. I was trying to build my strength up, and the ladies were there to make sure I kept on schedule. I still had no feeling in the lower part of my body, but I was stronger and feeling better every day. I just knew I'd be fine. It was only a matter of time before I'd be walking.

Steve wanted me to stay at the hospital in Denver until I had most of my strength back and then move to a training area in Virginia. Connie would have to leave by the end of the week to go back to classes. Her new term would be starting soon, and she would be back at Arizona State to finish her masters degree in education.

Gabriella was more than any man could ask for. She was always there to support me, and I knew that she loved me. I had wanted so long for a love like she gave me. I tried in every way to let her know I loved her, too.

"Jack, we've done just about all we can to this point. The problem with your lower body may take some additional surgery, but the best place for that is in Washington, D.C., at Veterans Hospital. So what I suggest is that we go ahead and get you out there. We'll have them drive you to D.C. from the airport. It's only about thirty minutes away. Their specialists are the best," Dr. Sterling told me. "I'm sure that you'll be fine."

"Dr. Sterling, I appreciate all you did for me here. I just wish you guys could be around when I do get to walk again. It's going to happen."

They flew me the following week to Virginia. The C-131 military plane was the same kind I had flown in while I was in Vietnam. The only difference was that in Nam, we were packed like sardines in the plane, to be taken to some further destination. This time it was all fixed up with hospital equipment, and had nurses and doctors. It actually looked like a large doctor's office on wheels. Gabriella hadn't flown on planes very often, and especially prop planes. They were a lot different, sound and sight.

"Are you sure we're going to make it in this thing?" Gabriella said.

"These things have been places that most people will never see. If this plane could talk, it would tell you about all the good and bad that took place in that war and probably more. Why don't you come lie down on this bed with me, and let's see if we can make a little history of our own," I said and pulled her over to me. She was smiling and I could tell by the look in her eyes that if there had been any way possible, we would have made love right then and there. We settled for holding each other, and continued with a kiss. It seemed as if even in the hard times this was a relationship that only grew stronger.

We landed in Virginia at 5:00 P.M. and two male nurses loaded me in my wheelchair. We went directly to an ambulance that was waiting for us, and took the short trip to Veterans Hospital, where I was to stay until I had recovered.

I was taken to a room on the tenth floor where I was surprised to see Steve, Gary, Cheryl and a doctor standing there.

"Well, my friend, I see you and Gabriella finally made it here," Steve said.

"Yeah, ole buddy, we were getting worried that you might stay there. Besides that, Cheryl is kicking my butt every day and I need you guys to help," Gary said.

"Gary, you're such a butt. I have just begun to work on you. You're really going to pay for that remark," Cheryl said.

"Gary, I thought by now that you would have learned not to mess with that girl," Gabriella said laughing.

"Well, I can't teach him everything," Cheryl said.

"I can't wait to get her on the basketball court," he continued.

"Jack, if you don't mind, I'd like for us to all go down to the cafeteria and have a quick meal and then discuss our plans for the next few weeks," Steve said.

"Could I have a few minutes to freshen up?" Gabriella asked.

"Sure, Gabriella, take your time. I just need to be on a plane by 10:00 tonight."

"Oh, we can make that easy, as long as Jack keeps his mouth shut," said Gary taking a poke at me.

"If I remember right, I was the one who had to shut you up so that we could get where we needed to be on time."

"I do believe it was the other way around. Remember the time—"

"Hey, can't we just get on with this? Cheryl and I are going to take charge now, and we'll do all the talking. You guys just have to learn how to listen," Gabriella interrupted as she high-fived Cheryl.

"I guess I might as well direct all my comments to the ladies and let them tell you two about it later," Steve said laughing.

Gary and I looked at each other for a second, then turned back to the ladies and said in unison, "Absolutely."

We made our way to the cafeteria and had a quick meal. After that, Steve led us to a conference room that was used by doctors at staff meetings. There was an oblong table in the middle of this large room with about twenty chairs surrounding it. It was made like furniture used to be made. Hardwood that must have been oak. The chairs were made of the same kind of wood and were on swivels. Big black cushions that showed very little sign of wear. We all found a place to sit. I was getting so good at this wheelchair thing that I slid out of it, onto the cushioned chair in one swift movement. Steve had a slide projector, and TV with a VCR set up by the chair he was sitting in.

"Well, ladies and gentlemen, it is time for you to meet the people that are causing all the trouble in California. I'll start from the bottom and work my way up the ladder. We know we have the right people and their places in the organization. The problem, as you know, is that we can't seem to get enough on them to break it up. That's where we hope you guys will come in and fix the problem. It's going to be dangerous, and we're not even sure that you can get in, but with a little luck."

Steve turned on the slide projector, and started running through picture after picture of people in the lower end of the organization. The ones who pass about a million dollars a year through their hands. The ones who also put it directly on the street. They were young high school kids to business executives in large companies. But to us, they were the little guys.

"Let me stop the slides for a minute, and show you a recent film that we have of the upper class. These were taken last week as they entered the house of the head guy."

What we saw was a mansion. It had to have at least fifty rooms, completely fenced in and protected by dogs, guards, and the latest security equipment. One by one, men and women got out of these very expensive cars and entered the house. Porsches, Jags, limos, and even a Rolls-Royce. In all, there must have been about ten people who went in the house. These were the people we were out to get.

"Now, watch very closely and you'll see the head man," Steve continued.

What I saw was a young Hispanic man, probably in his mid-twenties. Every hair was in place and his mustache was trimmed so that it made him look like a general in an old Spanish war movie. The kind that never actually fought in war, but just sat there on his white horse and gave the orders. There was enough gold around his neck to buy a new car. I could tell this guy was definitely in charge of everything. He was wearing knee-length shorts and a pullover shirt that had no collar.

"That is Mr. Willie Hernandez and he is the head man. Never had a conviction, and has a clean police record," Steve said. "The woman to the right is one of his girlfriends, Shani Wallace. Don't underestimate her. She is an expert with weapons and martial arts." She was about 5'4" and maybe a hundred pounds, but it was all put together perfectly. Long blond hair and blue eyes.

"Now, back to the slides. Here is the rest of the cartel. Tim Bell, Ined Morales, Vicky Burton, Derell Washington, and his second in command, Bill Torres. These are the people we want. These are the ones you guys are to get the evidence on. We hope you are anyway."

"How far down the line are we going?" Gary asked.

"We want everyone from bottom to top. If we work this right, I expect to have seventy-five to eighty arrested, and just as many convictions," Steve answered. "Now let me continue with the pictures. Everything that you are seeing on the slides happened in one afternoon. Just imagine the money that passes through this organization." He showed about thirty more frames, then leaned back in his chair. "Any questions guys?"

"Do you have a plan for us to get into the organization, or are we going to free-lance our way in?"

"I'm glad you asked that question. Gary, you are going to be the contact man. What I mean is, you will be the first one there, and start to set things up for Jack and Gabriella. You're going to explain that you have contacts with lots of money, and they will be moving in soon. We'll set Jack up at San Diego State and Gabriella in a local bank close to the campus. You'll be the assistant basketball coach at the same place, but you'll be heavily involved in the drug trade. Cheryl will be an English teacher there and dating you. That's the setup for now."

"Why this particular university?" Gabriella asked.

"There's a lot of drugs that go through it, and it's close to all the guys you'll be dealing with. Plus, where else would there be a better place for drugs to pass through than a university?" Steve stated.

"How long will it be before we start the move?" Gary asked.

"The spring semester doesn't start until February 14th, but we want Gary and Cheryl down there in about two weeks. If everything goes right, we want Jack and Gabriella down there by the end of the month as husband and wife. They'll move into a nice neighborhood, with all the looks of a normal family just moving to town."

Gabriella and I looked at each other, not knowing what to say or do. Marriage hadn't been thought about lately, because everything had been happening so fast. We turned our attention back to Steve.

"We hope to have everyone in place no later than February 1."

"That's Jack's birthday," Gabriella shouted.

"Great. Maybe we can have a little get together, and celebrate everything at one time," Gary said.

"Would that be all right, Steve?" Cheryl asked.

"Sure. You guys will need to be spending some time together anyway. Remember that Gary will have known you guys before, and even taught at the same school as Jack. That will work out fine."

"OK, then. We celebrate Jack's birthday at our new home," Gabriella said laughing.

"Well, that just about covers it for now. I'll let you guys get settled in here and be in touch with all of you again next week. Cheryl, you keep the training going with Gary and get Jack and Gabriella started, OK?"

"Sure Steve. That won't be a problem."

"I'll give you a call later tonight. Well, girls and boys, I have a plane to catch. It won't be long now. Things are starting to fall into place. Jack, get your act together soon," he said smiling.

"I plan to do just that."

"See you guys later. Cheryl, make sure these slides and stuff get put up, will you?"

"Sure thing, boss."

After Steve had gone, we all sat there for a few minutes just thinking about what we had just learned.

"I knew I had agreed to help break up a drug operation, but I hadn't realized it was this big. These guys must be selling a million dollars a week in an operation this large."

"We estimated that each one of the top guys in this operation are doing about half a million a week. That's a lot of drugs on the street," Cheryl continued.

"We sure have our work cut out for us," Gary said.

"I'm just glad the four of us will be working together," Gabriella said.

"Me, too," Gary said.

"I hate to break all of this up, but I'm getting a little tired. Can we continue all this tomorrow?"

"I'm sorry darling, we can go now," Gabriella stated.

"Let's get you back up to your room, and we'll be on our way," Cheryl said.

The hospital room they had for me had an extra bed in the corner so that Gabriella could stay with me. The only thing she would have to do is shower and change at the room they had for her at the agency. The private room I was to stay in was just like all the hospital rooms that I have ever seen. The TV hung from the ceiling, the bed was just a single, but I was sure that Gabriella and I could fit nicely in it.

"Jack, you do look tired. Are you all right?" Gabriella asked.

"I am tired, but I think it's mostly from the time change. I just need some rest."

"Why don't you lie down, and I'll ride over to the agency with Gary and Cheryl, get a quick shower, and come right back."

"That sounds great to me. I know I could sleep for a couple of hours. You go with them. I'll be all right."

"You will miss me, won't you?"

"Even in my sleep. I don't know how I existed without you all that time."

"Me either. Now close your eyes and sleep. Dream of me, will you?"

"Even before you leave."

They left the room, and it wasn't long before I had fallen into a very deep sleep.

The interesting thing was that I did begin to dream, and it was about Gabriella. When you love someone as much as I do her, it must be the natural thing to do.

14

*I*T WAS LATE AT NIGHT, AND WE WERE BACK IN FLORIDA in the parking lot of a lounge called Charlie's. The dream felt so real it was as if we were there. We had been inside having a quick drink before it was time for Gabriella to leave and go home. I had walked her to the car and had gotten in to talk with her for a few minutes before she left.

"I wish you could go out with me tonight."

"I'm with you right now. Doesn't that count for anything?"

"It's everything to me."

"There is an awful lot of light in this parking lot tonight. I think I'll find us a more dimly lit spot," and she drove to the darkest spot she could find. "This is much better. Now we can talk."

"Is this going to be a night where I can kiss you, or one that I can't?"

"That isn't fair, Jack. You know the only reason I won't let you is because I feel guilty. Plus, when I let you kiss me, I forget everything else."

"I know. I just thought I'd ask. It's much easier to ask than have you turn your head when I try."

"How about this for an answer?" She leaned over and kissed me very passionately on the lips. It was as if it had been years since we had been alone together. I held her very tightly and didn't want to let her go. Our tongues searched the inside of each other's mouth as we began to lose control. When we did part, I lowered my head and began to kiss her neck ever so gently. She leaned her head back so that I could enjoy every inch of her neck. I lowered my head even further to the first button on her blouse, and as if by command, I unbuttoned the top one, moving my kisses across the top of her breast. She sighed as I began to pull at her bra to explore more of her beautiful body. I kissed every inch of her breast that I could reach. She pulled my head back up and kissed me again. This time she did it with more intensity. Her tongue dashed in and out of my mouth. We were both loosing control. I lowered my hand, and gently placed it between her legs. She opened them so that I could slide my hand to the place I was sure it belonged. When I reached the middle of her magnificent body, she lunged forward, pushing at my hand as I moved it up and down the inside of her warm body. I could feel that she was becoming very wet, and we would either have to stop this soon, or the parking lot would not be safe for any passerby.

When we finally stopped for a minute, she said, "I have a surprise for you. I'm going out with you tonight."

"I'm not even going to ask how you managed that. I'm just glad you're here. Let's get out of this parking lot before they take us to jail."

"Jack, I don't really want to go dancing. I just want to be alone with you. Is that all right?"

"What a ridiculous question. You're in the driver's seat, and I'm all yours. I just need to drop my keys off with Billy Ray. He rode with me. Will you drop me off at Stingers later?"

"Sure. Just hurry up, will ya?"

I was in and out of Charlie's almost before she stopped the car.

"Where are we going anyway?"

"I thought maybe we'd take a walk along the beach. Is that all right with you?"

"We're not there yet!"

"It won't take long. You just have to be patient."

"I'm patient when I'm not with you," and I leaned over and kissed her neck. I kissed her again and again. She was maintaining control pretty well. I again slid my hand between her legs. With that, the car would speed up and slow down. I saw her loosing control, and I was enjoying every minute of it.

She took my hand and laughingly said, "If you don't stop, we're going to wreck. I told you to be patient."

We arrived at the beach shortly thereafter and parked. It was a beautiful clear night with a full moon. Thank goodness there weren't many people around. We got out of the car and began walking along the beach. We walked and held hands, stopping at times to hold one another and kiss. Then we'd continue our walk, laughing and talking about nothing and everything. It was a magnificent night. As we walked along, we saw an old drain pipe that was about three feet out of the ground. We sat there for a few minutes. She then got up and walked to face me. I opened my legs so that I could pull her between me. I started kissing her neck again and pushing as much as I dared against her. We kissed again and again. Once again I had unbuttoned her blouse and this time I had slid her strap down so that I could lower her bra low enough to reveal her nipple. I began to kiss it and caress it and kiss it more. It was hard and wonderful.

I moved back up to her neck, and then ear on my way to her cheek. I leaned back, took her face, and gently cupped it in my hands. I leaned forward so that I could kiss both of her eyelids and then her mouth.

"Let's go back to the car. This is all I can stand," she exclaimed.

We stood and started walking back to the car. I thought our evening might be over. Was I ever wrong. She drove the car along the beachfront until she found a spot that was secluded and very dark. She leaned over and kissed me, and before I knew it, she had climbed over the seat and was on top of me. I lowered the seat all the way back. I somehow had managed to take off my shirt, and her blouse and bra during the next few minutes. Her big beautiful breasts were now resting against my chest. I kissed her, then took one breast at a time, and kissed every inch of them. Before I knew exactly how she did it, she had managed to lower herself to the floorboard of the car, and began to unzip my pants. She took hold of the only part of my body that has no control. She caressed and kissed it until I could stand no more.

I pulled her to me again. She looked at me and said, "I want what's inside of you to be inside of me." The rest was the most wonderful and exciting night that I can remember. I exploded into an ecstasy that was beyond words. We became one that night.

"Did you have a nice rest, Jack?" I heard someone saying. I opened my eyes and Gabriella was standing over me. I grabbed her hand and pulled her close to me and kissed her.

"I'm glad you didn't get here five minutes earlier."

"Did I interrupt anything?"

"Remember the night at the beach? I was dreaming about it."

"It was wonderful, wasn't it? Do you remember those damned mosquitoes? I thought they were going to carry us away before we could get our clothes back on," she said laughing.

"I remember you still had welts on you the next day. I thought there was a bee hive in the car with us."

"Jack, I'd love to do it again," she said very seriously.

"I know we will. I just wish it was tonight."

"You don't mind if I lie down beside you, do you?"

"I can't believe you're not already here."

She slid in the bed with me, and we held each other very tight. She smelled wonderful and tasted even better.

"Jack, are you ready for this job that we're about to do?"

"You said the right word. It's a job and we're going to do it. We'll do it and be safe, and go on with our lives. You have nothing to worry about."

"Aren't you just a little worried?"

"For you and Gary and Cheryl, but other than that, I know we will do this. I just want you guys to be safe. Before, it was only me."

"As long as I'm with you, everything will be all right."

"Gabriella, you've been in my heart ever since that night at Charlie's. I'll never let you go again."

"You better never even try to get rid of me," she said laughing.

"I'd never do that. I couldn't pass up another night at the beach with you and the mosquitoes," I said as we both laughed.

We held each other close again and lay quietly in the bed. I ran my hands over as much of her body as I could. I wanted to feel the parts of her body that I used to feel lying next to her. I wanted the lower part of my body to respond and it wouldn't. I knew it would come in time, but I wanted it now. For the time being, I would have to be content. All I knew was that she was here with me and she loved me. We fell asleep in each other's arms.

15

"Jack, I think we should get married before we go out to California," I thought I heard Gabriella saying. "Jack, are you awake?"

"Did you know that I was having this wonderful dream about us and you woke me up?"

"Did you hear what I said?"

"Something about if I was awake. Why would I be awake at this time of night? What time is it anyway?" I said as I kidded her. I heard what she had said, but this was my attempt at humor at whatever time it was in the morning.

"It's four in the morning and I want to know what you think."

"I think it's too early to be awake. Couldn't you sleep?"

"Jack, I said I think we should get married before we go out to California. What do you think?"

"I think you're right," I said smiling at her.

"You heard me, you rat. You'll pay for that," and she began to tickle me.

"Hey, that's not fair. I can't fight back."

"Don't give me that stuff," and she began to tickle me even more.

"OK, I surrender. You're the better person, for now." I pulled her to me and kissed her. She was so warm and soft. Oh yeah, and mine.

"Seriously, don't you think we ought to get married?"

"Gabriella, I think you're absolutely right. I just have one small request."

"No request, Jack."

"I think we should wait till I get the movement back in my body."

"No way. Regardless, we set a day and we get married. All or nothing. That's the only deal I make."

"Just a minute ago you were asking me, and now you're making demands? Sounds like you're pretty sure of yourself."

"I know I don't have to make any demands. You've always been easy."

"Well, this time you're wrong. I have to be able to function. I won't burden you with half a man for the rest of your life."

"That's not going to happen and you know it."

I looked into her eyes, and she knew I was serious, then I said, "Gabriella, I'm really scared. I want to be well and I'm scared to death."

"That does it. I won't listen to anymore of this," she said and she got up out of the bed and walked to the window. I guess this was to be our first argument since we had been reunited.

"Gabriella, come back over here. Gabriella, I'm talking to you." She just stood there. She and I both knew she was going to win. What a wimp I am. "You win."

"Did you say something to me?" she said without looking at me.

"I said you win. Now, get your beautiful body over here to me."

She turned around, and looked at me with those big, beautiful, brown eyes and said, "Are you sure?"

"Would I kid with you? Now, get over here."

She hurried back to the bed and jumped under the covers with me. "Just marry me, Jack. Everything else will be OK." She then kissed me just like she did the first time. At least it seemed like it was just like it was our first kiss. I felt my heart racing, and I thought I felt my body responding. We kissed each other again.

"Can we go back to sleep now, or do you have any other demands you want to put on me?" I said playfully.

"Just one. That you promise to always love me."

"With all my heart. Always."

"Now you can go back to sleep." We just lay there holding each other and fell asleep again.

* * *

"It's time to wake up, big boy. We have a busy day ahead of us," I heard someone saying. "Wake up, mister. I have to take your temperature, and it's hard to do that when you're asleep."

I slowly opened my eyes, and saw this very tall nurse standing over me. She had a nice figure and long red hair that was almost hidden under her nurse's cap. She looked as though she could wrestle a bear for a living if she wanted to. "Who are you?" I said as I began to wake up.

"I'm Mrs. Steward. I've been assigned to you until we get you back on your feet again. That doesn't bother you, does it?"

"Not at all, Mrs. Steward. I was just asking. Have you seen Gabriella?"

"She went down to check on something. She'll be back in a minute. Now hold out your arm. I need to check your blood pressure."

"Do you talk to your husband this way?"

"Sure do."

"I thought so. Does he ever win any arguments?"

"Not many. Now, be quiet so I can get your blood pressure right. The doctor will be here soon."

"Do you mind telling me what the doctor's name is?"

"Not at all. I'm not that mean. His name is Rodriguez and he's one of the best in his field. If anyone can help you, he will."

"I'm sure he will. I just need to be walking soon. I have a very important engagement."

"I've already heard. With me working on you, it won't be long at all. If nothing else, I'll carry you to your wedding."

"She didn't waste any time telling somebody."

"That girl loves you a lot. You leave her alone, and let her enjoy it."

"I didn't mean it that way. She could tell the world if she wants too. In fact, if she doesn't, I will. By the way Mrs. Steward, I'm depending on you to help me be walking in time for my wedding, OK?"

"No problem, mister. We'll get it done."

"Guess what I've been doing?" Gabriella said as she finally came back to the room. She was smiling from ear to ear, and she looked like a million dollars. I knew she was happy about us getting married, but I hadn't realized that it would have this effect on her.

"I'm just glad you're back. I missed you when I woke up."

"Well, I'll have you know that I've been on the phone with Cheryl, then Gary, and finally, my parents. I had to tell someone or I was going to pop. I hope you don't mind."

"Would it matter if I did?"

"Of course it would, Jack. Now, do you mind that I've been telling everyone I could?"

"Does it make you happy?"

"What a dumb question. I couldn't be happier. Well, I was pretty happy the day I finally met you again at the concert. This is different. Now, for the last time. Do you mind?"

"Not at all."

"I knew you wouldn't. That's one of the great things about you. I think you're the most understanding and wonderful person I've ever known. By the way, I love you and good morning." She leaned over and gave me a very passionate kiss. If she could only know how much I loved her.

"Well, beautiful lady, what did they say?"

"Well, handsome man, I'm not going to tell you," she said playfully.

"Well, beautiful lady, I need to get some more sleep anyway. Wake me later, OK?"

"Jack, you can't sleep now. I have too many things to tell you about. Plus, we don't have much time. When I talked with Cheryl, she said that we were going to have one of the guys from the bureau working with us."

"Maybe with you., but not me. Mrs. Steward is giving me all I can handle right now. Are you sure she said both of us?"

"I'm positive. Don't change the subject. You can talk to the guy when he gets here."

"I thought you didn't want to tell me anything. Change your mind or something?"

That was the wrong thing to say. She grabbed me and started tickling me. I was fighting back, but not doing a very good job in my present condition. As she was tickling me, I thought I felt something in my legs. I'm not sure what it was, but there was some feeling there.

"Now, do we talk, or do I have to get really tough?" she said holding me down. Of course, I let her win. I really just wanted her near me. As she was leaning over, I raised up to kiss her and she playfully turned away.

"Not until you agree to talk about what we're going to do."

"OK. If you don't stop tickling me, I'm liable to overflow my pee bag." We began laughing and then she looked me in the eyes and again kissed me.

"I love you, Jack."

"I knew that," I said and tried to tickle her. Again I was losing.

"That does it, mister. Now you're in for it," and she started tickling me again.

"Wait. Stop, please. I love you, too. Now can we talk?"

"Maybe."

"Gabriella, I love you, and I'm happier than I could ever tell you. You're beautiful and wonderful and I'm the luckiest man alive."

"That's enough. You win. Let's talk."

"No, darling. We win. Now what did they say?"

"Since you insist, I guess I'll tell you. First I talked to Cheryl and she was very happy for us and excited. I asked her to be my maid of honor. Then, I called Gary and he congratulated us too. I think he wants to be your best man. He kind of hinted at that anyway. When I told my parents, I think they were a little surprised, but I told them that this is what I wanted and as usual, they were happy for me too. My sister went nuts. She was so excited. I told them they had to fly out for the wedding and they wanted to know how many people were going to come. I told them that I had to talk with our boss, and I'd get back to them when we had more information. By the way, Jack, you've made me very happy."

"I hope you can tell I'm happy, too."

"Jack, we are going to have such a great life together. I can't wait to be Mrs...whatever our last name is," she said and we laughed.

"It doesn't matter, does it?"

"Not as long as we're together. If it's OK with Steve, can I invite a bunch of my relatives? I want a big wedding."

"I don't care if the entire state of Florida comes, as long as you're there," and I raised up and gave her a big kiss.

* * *

"Good morning, you two. My name is Bill Whitehead and I'm going to start working with you both on some of the different equipment we'll be using for the case. Steve figured that wouldn't make the doctors go crazy, and we could get it done fairly easy."

"Nice to meet you, Bill. I'm Jack and this is my fiancée, Gabriella."

This guy was about thirty and had graying, short hair. He was about six-foot-three-inches tall and looked to be about two hundred pounds of a neatly put-together professional. He talked in a very deep voice. He shook hands with the both of us and said, "I just need to check with Dr. Rodriguez and make sure it's OK. Have you met him yet?"

"Not yet. Mrs. Steward, my nurse, said he should be making his rounds about nine."

"How about this then? I'll go grab a bite to eat and be back about nine-thirty. Would you make sure I get to see him before he leaves your room?"

"No problem, I'll come down and get you when he gets here to examine Jack," Gabriella said.

"Thank you," he said as he hurried out the door.

"I sure hope this guy can take a joke. He seems like he might be a little too much business for me," I said. I knew she was going to get me almost before I said it.

"Now, Jack. I think I remember you saying that we should never make first impressions of people. Remember?"

"I think I just might have created this monster. This monster who will remind me of everything I have ever said for the rest of my life."

"You shouldn't have taught me so well if you didn't want me to use it. By the way, if you don't like the way I am, we could always call off the wedding."

"Well, if that's what you really want...."

"I'll show you what I want," and she jumped on the bed, and kissed me while holding my arms down on the bed.

"Hey, that's not fair. I'm still a very sick man."

"You're not getting any sympathy from me, Mr. Cannon. The only thing you'll get from me is married."

I reached up, put my arm around her, and kissed her again. When I had finished, I said, "You're the best thing that ever happened to me. I can't wait until we're married."

"We haven't even set a date yet, have we?"

"Let's check with Steve first, and see what he can do to help us. He may not think it's such a great idea."

"He better, or we're out."

"I think you mean it."

"You know I do."

"And you know I agree with you." Then she kissed me again.

"I hate to break up what looks like a very exciting event, but I need to examine one of you. Unfortunately, I think it's this ugly guy you're holding down," this man said as we were still lying on the bed.

"You must be Dr. Rodriguez. I've heard a lot about you," I stated.

"It was all good, I hope."

"I haven't been here long enough to get all the real poop yet, but I'm working on it."

"I paid a lot of money to keep my name clean. You better not hear anything but the good. Now, Mr. Cannon, I need to do a brief examination of you. Do you think this lovely young lady will mind?"

"I'm sorry, we were only making a few plans. I'll be glad to move. I'm Gabriella. Jack's wife-to-be."

"Well, congratulations are in order. When's the big day?"

"We haven't set the date yet, but it has to be soon because of our schedule."

"It's nice to meet you. I wish the best for both of you. Now, I hope you don't mind if I ask you to leave the room while I examine your future husband. We need him one hundred percent for that day."

"I get the message and I don't mind. There's a man from the agency that would like to talk to you before you leave, and I have to go get him."

"Please ask him to hurry, because I have a lot of people to see today."

"I'll hurry," she said as she turned and left the room.

"Well now, Mr. Cannon, let's see just what we're up against," he said as he began to stick this little needle in my legs. Then he started moving my legs up to my waist. "Let me know when you feel something."

"You better believe I'll let you know. I'm tired of not being able to walk."

"You just have to be patient. Do you feel this?" He was poking me just above the kneecap.

"Nothing."

"Well, don't worry. I'm going to schedule some X-rays, and then I want to examine you again. I have the X-rays from the hospital you just left, but I'd like to see if anything's changed. Have you had any feelings at all since the accident?"

"Actually, I thought I had some feeling in my legs twice. Both times it was when Gabriella and I were fooling around. Do you think that it could be a signal of better things to come?"

"It was too early for that. Let's get the X-rays done and we'll see. It is definitely a positive sign, though. Just let me know if there are anymore."

"Is there a chance that I might start getting some feeling back soon?"

"It's way too early for me to talk yet, but from the X-rays I've seen, you don't seem to have any permanent damage. But for now, just relax. Mrs. Steward will give you all the exercise you need. Don't worry about anything. I'm sure we'll have you back to one hundred percent soon."

"I think the FBI wants me to start doing a little work with one of the agents. Something about surveillance equipment and different tactics that won't require much physical ability. Anyway, that's what the agent wants to talk to you about. He should be here pretty soon."

"Let's see what he has in mind, and I'll let you know. I don't want anything interfering with your therapy."

"Is there anything special you want me to do, Dr. Rodriguez?"

"Do exactly what Mrs. Steward tells you and everything will be fine. She'll be here soon to take you down for X-rays."

Just as he was about to leave, the agent arrived.

"Dr. Rodriguez, my name is Bill Whitehead, and I'm with the bureau. I think Mr. Fuller talked with you about Jack starting some light work."

He reached out and shook Bill's hand and said, "It's nice to meet you, Mr. Whitehead and yes, Steve did mention it. Check with Mrs. Steward and work around her schedule. If she thinks that it's putting too much strain on Jack, she'll let you know and you'll have to cut back. I see no problem as long as you don't try to do too much."

"Thanks Dr. Rodriguez, we need to get them both started as soon as possible," Bill said.

"Thank Jack. He's the one who has to do all the work. I've got to run now. See you all later. Jack, remember what I told you."

"No problem, Dr. Rodriguez, I know my limits. See you later."

"What did he say, Jack?" Gabriella asked.

"He told me that I should do whatever Mrs. Steward says and everything would be fine. I have to have some X-rays taken this morning and then he'll talk to me again. I'm not worried because the guy knows his stuff. I'm sure he wouldn't get my hopes up, and then not deliver."

"I can't wait till you're on your feet again. We still have some things to catch up on."

"You need to be careful what you say, Bill might think that's all we have on our mind."

"Don't worry about me. I know what you guys have been through and I want everything to work out for you both. Besides all that, I'll just take a break if you get out of hand."

We all laughed and then Bill stopped as if on command. He was a nice guy, but he needed to lighten up a bit. I said, "Bill, what do we do now?"

"Well, I plan to spend about two hours each morning with you and Gabriella. In the afternoon Gabriella will be working with Miss Hunter and Mr. Stevens. Of course, this is all subject to your approval."

"Sounds great to me. Jack and I are eager to get to work. I just need a little time each day to plan our wedding"

"I'm sure that won't be any problem."

"Could you get in touch with Steve, and let him know that we need to talk with him?"

"He'll be back in town tomorrow, and I'll let him know. Are you ready to get started?"

"Sure thing," Gabriella said.

For the next hour and a half, we saw equipment that I thought only existed in the movies. He started with cameras. There were very simple 35mms to very high-powered ones that could watch an ant clean his face from two hundred yards away. We could even see you breathing in your sleep. Next it was the listening devices. Everything from the smallest hidden stick pin to the stuff that they use in telephone listening and tracking of calls. It was great stuff. We even saw the newest thing in secret listening devices for a two-way conversation. It's implanted in the base of the throat for talking and in the ear lobe for listening. Really amazing stuff.

"Jack, I need to get you down to therapy now. Are you guys through?" Mrs. Steward asked.

"That's probably enough for our first day anyway. We'll meet at ten tomorrow if that's all right with you, Mrs. Steward," Bill said.

"That's fine Mr. Whitehead. How long will he need to be with you each day?"

"About two hours if that's possible."

"That should be all right. I'll let you know if there's any problem. OK, Jack, let's get you downstairs. Gabriella, we shouldn't be long."

"Thank you, Mrs. Steward."

"Just call me Shirley. Let me know if there's anything I can help with when you start planning the wedding. I know where everything is in town. OK?"

"I'll appreciate anything you could do. I don't know anything about this place."

"I'll just spend part of my day beating up on your future husband and the rest is yours."

"Thanks again, Shirley."

"You're welcome. Now Jack, hold on, 'cause here we go."

"Hey! What were you? A race car driver in your first life?"

"No time to waste. You'll get used to it."

"I sure hope so. Do you drive your car this way too?"

"You bet!"

During the next two hours Shirley worked on every part of my lower body. There was massage and exercise equipment, and they were all used on me. She was very demanding, but there was also a kindness about her that she didn't want anyone to see. I'm sure that comes with the many years of good and bad that she's seen.

"How much are we going to do today, Shirley? I'm getting really tired."

"We're just about done, Jack. You didn't say anything about feeling any sensation in your legs. Did you feel anything?"

"In my left leg, I thought I felt something in the back calf, but it went away and I never felt anything else."

"Well, just keep me informed. OK? Now, let's get you back to your room so you can rest."

16

WHEN I GOT BACK TO THE ROOM, I found a note from Gabriella saying that she had gone to work with Cheryl and would be back soon. It was almost 3:00 P.M. and I was extremely tired, so I closed my eyes for a little nap. When I woke up, I saw Gabriella sitting there in the corner, with tears in her eyes. She looked beautiful and I wanted her badly.

"What's wrong, darling? I hope I haven't done anything to make you unhappy."

"I was just thinking about the night we spent together after I hadn't seen you for about two weeks. Remember that we stayed at a friend's house? I can't even remember his name, but I remember the night like it was yesterday. Making love to you that night was wonderful. You were so warm, and I loved falling asleep next to you. Do you remember?"

"I remember that you took advantage of my weakened state and I lost control. That was very unfair and I loved every minute of it."

"Not that part. The part where we woke up next to each other, and you held me very close. It was the first time we actually spent the night together."

"Gabriella, it was the very best night ever, and I'll never forget it. I love you. One of these days we'll relive every minute of it. I have no intention of staying this way the rest of my life."

"Don't worry, Jack. You'll be chasing me down the halls soon. I just know it."

"Thanks for being here for me. I don't know what I'd have done without you."

"How many times have I told you that you don't have to thank me. We're beyond the thank you and I'm sorry response."

We talked for another hour or so. Then Gabriella laid down beside me and we fell asleep. She is the most warm and passionate woman I have ever met. God made us for each other.

* * *

When I awoke the next morning, Gabriella was already gone. There was a note that said, "I'll be back soon. Making wedding plans. Love you, Gabriella." She was so excited, and I was glad she was so positive about everything. I needed that now. I had only heard bits and pieces of the plans she was making, but it sounded like it was going to be a very big and wonderful wedding. I was brought back to reality when the nurse came in and wheeled me off to therapy. The work out went as usual and was over in no time. I came back to have breakfast with Gabriella, and then we began our training with Bill. Then came the afternoon session of therapy. That too went as usual, until we were just about finished.

"Mrs. Steward, I definitely felt some tingling in my toes."

"Which leg, Jack?"

"Both of them."

"Let me get Dr. Rodriguez on the phone, and see if he wants to examine you. Don't run off anywhere 'til I get back," she said laughing and heading towards the phone. She returned in a minute or two, and said that Dr. Rodriguez would be there in a few minutes. "Gabriella will be very excited about this."

"Mrs. Steward, we aren't going to tell her anything about this until I'm able to walk to her."

"Are you sure that's what you want to do? Seems a little unfair to me."

"I want to surprise her, and besides, this may not be anything. You have to promise me that you won't say a word."

"Jack, I won't say anything as long as you let me help with whatever plans you have with the surprise."

"Agreed."

"Dr. Rodriguez, is this a good sign or what? Do you think I could be close?" I said as he entered the room.

"How about giving me time to examine you first? I know you're excited, but calm down," he said as he began to examine me. It only took him a couple of minutes and he was done.

"Dr. Rodriguez, it's starting to go dead again. I can't feel anything at all now. Was it just my imagination?"

"Jack, I warned you that this might happen. Don't look like that. This is the first stage of getting feeling back into your legs. It shouldn't be long now. Just keep up the exercise and let nature take its course."

"Whatever you say. I guess I got a little excited."

"You have a right to be excited; it won't be long now. Gabriella will be ecstatic. When is she due back?"

"I don't want to tell her yet. When I can walk to her, then I'll tell her. OK?"

"Sounds good to me. Mrs. Steward, are you in on this too?"

"He made me promise."

"She'll probably shoot all of us, but it's going to be exciting watching her face."

"Thanks, Dr. Rodriguez."

The next few weeks went by quickly for all of us. We had been through the same routine every day except Sunday, and all of us were learning a lot. Gabriella and Gary were just about ready, and I had done all I could in my limited capacity. Gabriella had been very busy with the wedding arrangements, and had recruited Cheryl, Gary, and Mrs. Steward to help. Everything was getting close, and everyone in the hospital was excited.

"I think I'll be ready for the wedding. What do you think, Mrs. Steward?"

"If things keep going the way they are now, you'll be ready by the end of the week. Has she suspected anything yet?"

"If she has, I haven't noticed. She's been so busy with the wedding and her training, that she hasn't had much time for anything else."

"We'll pull it off. She'll be so happy. I can hardly wait. It's only two weeks to the wedding. Are you getting excited yet?"

"I can hardly wait. I'm so much in love with this woman. I thought nothing could be better, but being married to her has to be the highlight of my life."

17
Gabriella

IT WAS NOW FRIDAY. Only two more days before Jack and I would finally be married. I was so excited. He was everything that I had ever wanted and I loved him more every day. I had only one wish—that he would be walking to me. It didn't matter though, just as long as we were married.

I did have a couple of surprises for him that I hoped would make him happy. While making arrangements with Connie to be at the wedding, she told me about Kevin. Kevin is Jack's son, and they hadn't spoken to one another in five years. They had a major blowup about his divorce, and hadn't even tried to communicate since. It must have been pretty bad, because in all the time I had known Jack, he never mentioned his son. Well, so much for that. Connie and I together had convinced Kevin to come. It wasn't easy, but we did it.

The other surprise, and I mean big surprise, was that I had contacted Michael Bolton and he had agreed to sing at our wedding. Plus, he had talked Kenny G into coming along. Steve had to add some extra security, and check out all the band members. The usual stuff that FBI people do. He also had to make sure that no media people would get wind of this. This wedding was going to be one that should have a book written about it. Just two more days.

On the following day, I picked my family up from the airport. "Well, Gabriella, tomorrow is the day you've been waiting so long for. Are you sure you're ready?" my mom asked.

"Mom, I can't tell you how ready I am, or at least I can't put it into words. We have a lot to do today. I hope you got plenty of rest."

"How's Jack doing?" my dad asked.

"He's fine. There's no change in his condition, but he's strong and very excited. I really think he's more excited than me, if that's possible."

"I can't wait to see the dress you're going to wear. What does mine look like?" my sister asked.

"You'll see soon enough, so don't ask anymore questions. As soon as Connie gets here, we'll all go down for the final fitting. You guys are going to love his daughter. I don't know anything about his son, so I guess we'll all get to meet him together."

"What son?" my mother, surprised.

"I'm sorry, Mom. In all this excitement, I forgot to tell you about Kevin." I filled them in with as much as I knew about him.

"Why didn't Jack tell you about him?" my dad asked.

"Connie said that he never even mentions him. It must have been very serious. Jack doesn't even know he's coming. I'm sure he'll explain it to me later. I just want them to get back together again."

"I hope this doesn't backfire on you," my dad said.

"Nothing is going to go wrong. I know everything will be perfect."

"How many people did you end up with that will be here for the wedding?" my sister asked.

"I think about fifty when I finally got through. It's hard to know exactly, because I think the whole staff at the hospital will be there. They never had anything like this happen before. With Michael Bolton and Kenny G being here, it's been almost impossible to keep it quiet, but we've done a pretty good job."

"I can hardly wait to meet them. You will introduce me to them, won't you Gabriella?" my sister asked.

"If you promise to behave, and not drool all over them."

"We haven't had a fight in years. I'd hate to give you a black eye before your wedding," she said.

"Just calm down. I've arranged for you to meet them. Besides that, you'll be the one with the black eye. I can still kick your butt."

When we arrived at the hotel and settled in, my mother, father, and sister went to some of the rooms to talk to the relatives that had already arrived. I had to go back to the hospital to see Jack, and make sure he was OK. I had already arranged for Gary to pick up Connie and Kevin at the airport, so at least that was taken care of. There were so many things left to do, and so little time. I was sure that there had to be something I was forgetting. Talking with Jack would help me calm down. It always does.

18

*W*ELL, HELLO STRANGER. How about telling me something," Jack said as I leaned down and gave him a kiss.

"Hello yourself. Tell you what?"

"Are we getting married or divorced? I haven't seen much of you lately. I miss you, and can we do this in a hurry so we can be together again?"

"Jack, I'm sorry, but this is the most important day of my life, and I want everything to be perfect. Don't you?"

"Quit looking at me like that. You know I was only kidding. We'll have plenty of time together later. You do what you have too. I just want you to remember that I love you," he said as we kissed again.

"Jack, this is the last chance you have to change your mind. Any regrets?"

"None, and don't ask again. I've wanted this since the first time we met. Do you have any regrets?"

"I just wish that you could walk to me. It won't affect the wedding, but I just wish that for you."

"Don't worry darling, it will be a beautiful wedding, and everything will be perfect. Besides that, I'm marrying the most beautiful woman in the world. Who could ask for more?"

"OK, enough of that. I have to leave you for a while, and make sure all the plans I have made are carried out. I'll be back a little while later with my parents and sister. Connie will be by later, too. You just try and get some rest. You'll need all your strength for tomorrow. OK?"

"Don't worry about me. I'm ready. Just do what you have to do and I'll be fine," he said as I gave him a big hug and kiss as I was about to leave.

I walked outside to where the wedding was going to take place to make sure everything was in order. We had selected a spot outside the hospital where there was plenty of room for the guests including the staff members. There had been a platform built between two huge oak trees, and it looked to be decorated and ready. There were flowers everywhere, and everything was blue and white. Off to one side there was another platform built where Michael Bolton and Kenny G's bands were to be stationed, and it looked ready. The chairs were all set up in front of the platform, and to the rear and off to one side was a large tent where the reception was to be held. There were a couple of workmen still doing a few minor things, but for the most part, it was as ready as it could be.

"What do you think, Gabriella?" I heard a voice say from behind me. It was Mrs. Steward.

"You have done a beautiful job, Shirley. Thank you so very much." And I gave her a hug.

"You two deserve it, Gabriella. The agency was a big help when they sent all those people over. Be sure and thank Steve."

"Oh, I will. We couldn't have pulled this off without Steve's help."

"Are you all set over at the hotel? I mean with your gown, and all the bridesmaids' gowns?"

"I think so. I'm on my way over there now to double check. Want to come along?"

"If you don't mind waiting about fifteen minutes for my shift to end."

"Not at all. I'll just walk around and look things over one more time."

"Great! I'll be back in just a few," and she was off.

I walked down the center aisle, and up on the platform, then turned around and looked back. I tried to imagine what it would be like tomorrow. My heart began to beat very fast, and I got very excited. Tomorrow at this time, I would be Mrs. Jack Cannon. I could hardly wait. I looked up at the floor that Jack's room was on, and saw him looking down at me. Gary walked over to the window, too. They both started to clap their hands to embarrass me. I just smiled and waved at them. I felt tears beginning to run down my cheeks. This was going to be the very best day of my life.

"Are you ready, Gabriella?" I heard Shirley say.

"Yes. Just look at those two clowns up there."

She turned and looked up. They were still applauding.

"That man sure loves you."

"Yes, I know. I love him, too."

"Let's get out of here before I start to cry myself."

We walked down the platform, waved one more time, and headed for the hotel.

As we were entering the hotel, Shirley said, "Have your relatives and guests arrived?"

"All of my family and Jack's son and daughter are here. Michael Bolton and Kenny G won't fly in until early in the morning. They are both doing shows tonight."

"It seems as though everything is just about ready. You've done a great job for the amount of time you've had to prepare."

"I never could have done it without you and the others."

"I am just as excited as you are. This is going to be a wedding that none of us here at the hospital will ever forget."

"I know I'll never forget it. I can hardly wait."

"It's almost over now," Shirley said as we opened the door to my room.

As we entered the room, I saw my mother making final adjustments to my sister's gown. My cousins were trying their dresses on, and were standing on one side of the room laughing and having a good time. My sister's gown was a very pale blue and trimmed in white. She was to be my maid of honor. She was beautiful, and the gown was stunning.

"You look beautiful, Stephanie. Does it fit all right?"

"It's just right. This gown is gorgeous. Who picked them out?"

"Shirley helped me. She has great taste, wouldn't you say?"

"A lot better than yours."

"Ha! You're going to pay for that one. By the way, this is Shirley Steward. She not only helped with most of the wedding plans, but she's also Jack's nurse."

I took her around the room and introduced her to everyone. She already knew Cheryl and Connie, but she hadn't met my mom, sister, and two cousins that were to be the bridesmaids. They were all in their gowns and were beautiful. My dad and Kevin were watching a football game on the TV.

"Gabriella, go in the other room, and put on your gown so we can see what it looks like," my mother commanded.

"Shirley, could you give me a hand?"

"Sure."

After five or so minutes, we came out of the room with Shirley holding my train off the floor. My dress was white, of course, low cut in the front, with two thin straps that crossed over my shoulders and connected in the back. There was lace everywhere. After being skin tight to my hips, it flared out from there down. The train was about five feet long. The gown seemed to highlight my figure, but still looked very feminine and soft. The veil covered my face, and fell over my shoulders in the back.

"Gabriella, I have never seen you look more beautiful," my dad said.

"Thanks, Dad. It couldn't be that you're just a little blind, because I'm your daughter."

"He's right, Gabriella, you're very beautiful," my mom said.

Everyone started to applaud. It almost embarrassed me. I decided to just curtsey and say thank you.

"OK, that's enough. Dad, have you and Kevin tried on your tuxes yet?"

"They're perfect."

"Great."

Later on, after dinner, we all went back over to the hospital to visit with Jack for a little while. Connie and I went in to see Jack first because we wanted to tell him that Kevin was here. We had no idea how he would take it, but Connie and I figured we could handle him and soften him up.

"Hi, honey, did you miss me?"

"It's about time you got back here. Hi, Connie, get over here and give me a kiss."

"Hi, Dad. I missed you," she said as she leaned down and kissed him on the cheek.

Then I did the same and whispered, "I love you."

"I'm glad you guys are here. Gary was driving my crazy."

As he said that, Gary came out of the bathroom. "Hello ladies. Don't let him kid you. His team lost their football game today, and that's why he's upset. Of course, I won ten bucks off him."

"Haven't you learned not to bet against him yet?"

"I didn't think Alabama would get beat by Florida."

"You're kidding, Dad," Connie said.

"Unfortunately, I'm not."

"Enough about football. Jack, Connie and I need to talk to you for a minute about something important. Gary, could you go down and keep my family company for a few minutes?"

"No problem. I can take a hint," he said as he left the room.

"Now, what's this all about? I know I'm going to lose with both of you here."

"Dad, please don't get upset, but...."

I interrupted, "Jack, it was my idea, and I want you to promise that you won't get upset when we tell you."

"Nothing is going to upset me on the day before our wedding. Now, what is it?

"OK. You promised. Kevin is here," Connie said.

His expression didn't vary one way or the other when he said, "Go get Kevin, and tell him I want to see him. Give me a few minutes alone with him. OK?"

"Jack, you promised."

"Everything will be fine, Gabriella. I promise."

We went down to the waiting room, and told Kevin that his dad wanted to talk with him. He came back in about ten minutes, and asked that we all come down to the room. I couldn't get any indication of how it went from the expression on his face.

"We have a confession to make," Jack said with a smile on his face. "Kevin and I talked on the phone a couple of days ago when I invited him to the wedding. We decided to keep it a secret until now. Don't you guys beat us. We just wanted to surprise you."

Connie and I ran over to Jack, and punched him a couple of times, then we tickled him. Everyone was happy and laughing.

"Jack, be glad we're all in such a good mood or you'd really pay for that one."

"Yeah, Dad, that wasn't very nice," Connie said. We all talked about the wedding for a couple of hours and then I asked everyone if I could have a little time alone with him before visiting hours were over.

"I was getting tired anyway," my dad said.

"I think we all need some rest," my mother continued. "We'll see you tomorrow, Jack." She hugged him and gave him a kiss.

With that, they all left, and Jack and I were finally alone.

"It won't be long now. I hope your...."

"Don't even say it," Jack interrupted before I could even finish. "You and I know that this was meant to happen for us. Let's just leave it at that. OK?"

"Your right, and I do know it. I also know that I love you with all my heart."

"I love you the same way, Gabriella."

"I can hardly wait."

"Do you know all your lines in our wedding vows?"

"They're the most beautiful I ever heard Jack, and you did better than anyone could at expressing how we feel about each other. Thank you for loving me."

"No...thank you for loving me."

We talked for a while longer, and I left to try and get some sleep.

19

*T*HE SUN WAS SHINING THROUGH THE WINDOW in my room in the hospital when Mrs. Steward came in and woke me up.

"It looks like it's going to be a beautiful day for your wedding, Jack."

"Was there ever any doubt? What are you doing waking me up so early? It's only seven."

"We need to do a very quick exam, and a short session of therapy before everyone starts getting here. Dr. Rodriguez will be here in a little while. Gabriella still has no idea that you're walking, does she?"

"None at all. We've done a pretty good job of hiding it, wouldn't you say?"

"She is going to be so happy."

"Well, Jack, today's the big day. Are you ready?" Dr. Rodriguez said as he entered the room.

"I've been ready all week."

"Have you had any problems with the feeling in your legs or anything?"

"None at all. Everything seems to be back to normal."

"Well, I want to look at you real quick, and Mrs. Steward wants to put you through a short workout. That should be enough for today."

His examination lasted about five minutes, and everything seemed to be OK. Mrs. Steward wheeled me to the therapy room and put me through a fast and hard workout. No problem, I was getting stronger every day.

With that completed, she wheeled me back to my room. The kitchen had sent up a special breakfast, and even had one of the staff serve it to me in bed. Everyone was being so nice. I ate my breakfast in record time, and took a quick shower. I didn't want anyone to catch me up and walking around. Just as I was drying off, Gary came walking in the room.

"Good morning, Jack. Are you ready? Hey man, when did this happen?"

"Get in here and close the door before anyone else comes in. It happened a couple of weeks ago, and I've been keeping it a secret to surprise Gabriella."

"Well, you did a good job, because none of us even had a suspicion. Has all the feeling returned or what?"

"Everything is back to normal. I'm still a little weak, but besides that, I'm one hundred percent."

"Gabriella is really going to be shocked. She might even beat the crap out of you when she finds out," he smiled.

"I don't think so."

"You're right. She'll just be so happy to see you walking. Besides, it's your wedding day. I guess there's going to be a hot time tonight. Is that part of your equipment working, too?"

"It better, or I'll take a hammer to it. Seriously, I'm not sure, but we'll give it a try."

"I'll bet...." he laughed.

"What are you doing here so early?"

"I wanted to make sure you had everything you needed and help you get ready. What you might need now is just to make sure nobody catches you walking around."

"We still have about four hours until the wedding. You could have waited 'til later to come over."

"To tell you the truth, I couldn't sleep, and I was sure you'd be up. Did you get any rest?"

"Not much. This is making me nervous, and I never get that way. I just want everything to be perfect so Gabriella will remember this day forever."

"Women don't forget anything. Haven't you learned that yet?"

"Yeah, but they're a lot easier to live with if the things they do remember are good ones."

"You're right."

"I just hope I don't forget the lines when it's my turn to speak. I'm sure Gabriella will do hers perfectly, and I don't want to mess up."

"You'll do just fine. Just remember that you wrote the lines— you have no excuse."

"Thanks, ole buddy."

"When do you plan on walking? Before or after the vows?"

"I plan to wait until Gabriella has read her part, and then stand to read mine. Does that sound like about the right time to you?"

"She might get excited if you do it then. Maybe you should wait until he pronounces you man and wife."

"Sometimes you surprise me, and come up with good ideas," I said, and we both laughed.

"I think we should have a little toast to your wedding. What do you think?"

"Sounds good to me. What did you bring with you anyway?"

"Jack Daniel's. What else?"

"That means we can only have one drink, or we will be in trouble."

"That's all we need until after the wedding," he said as he pulled the bottle from his bag.

We had our shot of JD, and sat around talking until it was time to start getting ready. People kept coming by to say good morning and to wish us well. I looked out the window and noticed that people were milling around already, waiting for things to get started. Everything was beautiful. Mrs. Steward, and everyone who helped, had done a wonderful job at getting everything ready in such a short time. I noticed a big semi-truck unloading stuff for the band. I didn't know where they got the band, but it was very well organized; they were just about ready. I had already started getting dressed, and Gary was ready and looked more nervous than I felt. Gabriella's father had come by, and told me everything over at the hotel was going fine. Kevin had joined us in the room now, and we were just sitting around waiting. It seemed as time got closer, it got further away.

By 12:30, I had done everything I could to make myself look good. It's a good thing Gabriella thought I was handsome, because I looked at myself in a mirror and just laughed. I definitely got the better end of the deal. I sat in the wheelchair, and Gary started pushing me out of the room. We went to the elevator and down to the first floor. They had arranged for us to go around the side of everything to avoid the people who were everywhere. I couldn't understand how such a small event had turned into a concert-like atmosphere. Anyway, we made our way around to the back of the platform where there was a small crowd gathered. I saw the preacher talking to two guys with long hair. People were gathered around them. Then I finally recognized the two guys, and realized that this was why all the hospital staff was there.

I turned to Gary, "Did you guys know that Michael Bolton and Kenny G were going to be here?"

"I guess you weren't the only one who had a surprise," Gary said.

"You must have been the only one who didn't know," Gabriella's dad continued.

"That sure explains why all the people are here."

"It was really hard to keep it out of the press, but the agency did a good job. Only the hospital staff and the people that Gabriella invited are allowed anywhere near here. There are FBI agents everywhere," Gary said.

"I'm glad the whole town didn't know or we wouldn't have been able to get my wedding done at all. You guys had better get wherever it is you need to be. I'll be all right here."

With that, Kevin, Gary, and Mr. Newman headed off. I made my way up to where the preacher and my surprise guests were waiting.

Michael turned and walked towards me, and the whole crowd of people followed. "Jack, it's great to see you again. I hope you're feeling up to this wedding."

"I wasn't expecting to see you here. I see Gabriella's been up to her tricks again. How did she get you here anyway?"

"She just called and asked. I wouldn't have missed it for the world. I want to introduce you to my wife, Karen, Kenny G, and you met my agent, Joe," he said. "Everyone, this is Jack, the husband to be, and half the reason we're all here."

I began to shake hands with them. "It's nice to meet all of you. I still can't believe you're all here. Thank you so much for coming. You all are helping to make this a wedding that Gabriella and I will never forget."

Kenny G said, "It's our pleasure. Besides that, Michael promised me dinner."

"Thank you, Kenny. If I may call you that."

"Please do."

"You can all talk later, gentlemen. We must get into position now," the preacher said.

"Right. Jack, let me help you get up on the platform."

"Thanks, Michael."

With that, everyone headed for his or her designated spots. It was almost time to begin. On the platform with Michael Bolton and his wife, was his and Kenny G's agent, the preacher, and myself. Kenny G had joined the band off to the right. I looked toward the back of the area, and noticed that everyone was still inside the hospital doors. I knew it wouldn't be long now. The whole place was full of people. Not only were all the chairs full, but people were standing down both sides of the row of chairs. It was a sight that I hoped someone was getting on film. I noticed that off to one side there was a huge camera on a platform. It looked more like a TV camera than a home-movie type.

I looked over at Michael and he said, "I wanted to make sure we got this all on film. I brought my own cameraman along. I'll make sure you get a copy."

"Thanks again, Michael. You didn't have to go to all that trouble."

"No trouble at all."

The doors swung open to the hospital and people started coming out the door. Finally, I got a glimpse of Gabriella standing just inside, and her mother and a relative were adjusting something on her gown. Within a few seconds, her father was along side of her, and everything was set.

Kenny G's band was playing the wedding song. I saw Cheryl and Gary walking out the door followed by Connie and Steve. Then came two of Gabriella's cousins escorted by two FBI agents. When they reached their places, they all turned and faced the rear of the grounds where Gabriella and her father were standing. It was the most beautiful setting that anyone could ask to have a wedding. Everyone had turned to watch the bride. It became very quiet—so quiet, that I could hear the birds talking to each other in the trees.

Again Kenny G raised his sax and began to play the wedding march as I had never heard it played before. Gabriella and her father walked out of the shadows of the hospital doors and started towards the front of the grounds. As the sun hit her, it revealed the most stunning woman I had ever known. She was a goddess in white. The veil covered her face, but her beauty couldn't be hidden. Her smile could be seen as the sunlight shown on her. This was a picture right out of heaven. The train on her veil and gown fell off her shoulders, as she seemed to glide towards the front of the grounds. The setting was great, the music was magnificent, and the woman was the most beautiful person God had put on this earth. I could hear the people sighing as she passed where they were standing. As she got closer and closer, my heart began to beat out of control. This woman would be my wife soon, and I couldn't believe it was happening.

As Gabriella and her father reached the front of the grounds and walked up the platform, I looked at Michael Bolton one more time and whispered, "Thank you." He just smiled back at me, and I could tell he was impressed.

We all turned and took our places on the platform. As the preacher went through the ceremonial words, everyone listened very intently. Then he turned to us and asked if we would say our vows. As he said that, I only hoped that what I had written and rehearsed would or could express the feelings I had in my heart at this very moment.

Gabriella and I faced each other. I began what I hoped would be something that she would remember forever. "This day in my life has been planned since I first saw you. We were meant to be together, and I just want to express to you what God has put in my heart. I promise to you that I will give you every ounce of my being. That I will care for you as no other has been or ever will be. I promise that with the help of God, you will be the first thing I think about when I awake and the last thing when I fall asleep at night. Any dream that I dream while sleeping will include you. Darling, I promise you all the love that I have now or will ever have. With all that in mind, I turn my heart over to you to care for. Accept this ring as the mold that bonds us together forever."

Gabriella squeezed my hand as I finished, and I could feel her pulse in her fingers. She began as soon as I finished. "This day in my life was also planned, and God has given me these words to say to you so that you will know they are sincere. I promise that as we exchange the love in our hearts and mold them into one, it will be God's hands that have shaped it. I promise that I will care for you as no other can or will. I promise you love beyond belief. I will always be yours, and you will always be mine. When God takes us away, it will be together, as we will only exist as one from this day forward. Accept this ring as the completion of the mold that bonds us together."

"With these words of love and commitment, I pronounce you man and wife. You may now kiss the bride," the preacher said.

With that I stood up, and pushed back the wheelchair. I reached out and lifted the veil that was covering all this beauty. As I did, I saw her crying, and smiling at the same time. She was the most beautiful woman in the world. I leaned forward, put my arms around her, and kissed her. After a few seconds, I whispered in her ear, "I love you, Gabriella."

"Jack, I love you too. When did you start walking? Never mind. I love you. This is the greatest moment in my life and I thought it couldn't get better."

"It's only the beginning, Mrs. Cannon."

"I know, darling," she said as she kissed me again, and everyone applauded and cheered.

As we turned and faced out at the crowd, Michael stood and began to sing. We walked down the stairs of the platform, and Gabriella and I turned around and listened as Michael sang his song. It was the best I had ever heard him sing it. Either that or it was the fact that he was singing it to Gabriella and me.

Michael sang a couple more songs, and then we began to make our way to the reception area. Everyone was hugging, kissing and crying. I thought I'd have my hand shook off.

The hospital staff and the agents that helped with the reception had done a great job. Everything was perfect. It lasted until the wee hours and everyone had a great time. Michael Bolton and Kenny G had to leave around 6:00 P.M., but gave us a copy of the wedding film before they left. I kept giving subtle hints to Gabriella that we should go to my hospital room and then sneak back. It didn't work, and of course I knew it wouldn't. We had a nine-tier cake, compliments of the hospital caterer. It was blue and white and beautiful. We had everything that could make a wedding unforgettable and more. Gabriella and I would never forget this day as long as we lived. Everything had worked as planned and the world was a beautiful place. No one would ever take this away from us.

20

*I*T SEEMED LIKE WE WOULD NEVER BE ALONE. I thought I couldn't possibly wait any longer. Finally, Steve came over and saved us. He had another surprise for us that neither Gabriella or I had any idea was going to happen.

"Jack, I have something special planned for you and Gabriella. Everything is all set," he said as he handed us a key.

"Steve, you've done enough for us already," Gabriella said.

"Yeah, Steve, we have everything we need."

"You guys deserve it. We'll have the family over there tomorrow night for a little party. Just enjoy it tonight and tomorrow. We turned off all the surveillance cameras, so don't worry," he said laughing.

"OK, boss, where do we go?"

"Right around the far side of the hospital," Steve said as he pointed around the east side of the hospital.

Everyone that was still there started walking in the direction he had indicated. As we went around the side of the building, I saw part of the surprise he was talking about. It was a helicopter. Not a small one, but the kind that you see the president getting out of on TV. He even had the red carpet rolled out for us. We still had no idea where we were going, but we knew we were going to fly there. It took us about ten minutes to finally get in the chopper, because everyone had to say a tearful good-bye. It was more than Gabriella and I had planned for or ever imagined. As the door closed to the helicopter, it seemed such a sad moment. I hated to see this fantastic day come to an end. Gabriella was crying and waving as the chopper took off from the pad.

"Jack, this day is going to be something that we'll never be able to top. You know that don't you?"

"Gabriella, it'll give me something to shoot for. Besides, this is a day that we'll never forget."

"I'll never forget it. I'll also never forget how much I love you. Just wait 'til I get you alone."

"Have something in mind, do you?"

"It's been entirely too long, and I owe you for not telling me about being able to walk."

"I wanted to surprise you. Did I do a good job?"

"I think I did a pretty good job of surprising you, too. Michael and Kenny G were so glad to come. They were great, and yes, you surprised me. I almost fainted, but I was happy."

As the helicopter continued its flight to wherever we were going, Gabriella and I held each other and talked about how great everything had worked out. Her family had been so understanding and helpful. Even her dad, who was against it at first, turned out to be very understanding after he and I had a long talk. He was only concerned about our age difference. After I explained that most marriages aren't lasting very long and wouldn't he rather have his daughter happy for say twenty or twenty-five years as opposed to three or five, he agreed. I promised him that I would never be anything but the very best I could for his daughter.

The helicopter was landing on an island off the coast of Virginia. I had no idea what it was or where. There were buildings everywhere and people all about.

"Excuse me, sergeant, do you have any idea where we are?" I asked the Army guy who rode with us.

"Yes, sir. This is an island resort that was built for the higher-ups from Washington. Only the bigwigs come here. You guys must be pretty important to be here."

"Not very important, I'm afraid. Just very lucky to have friends that are. Where do we go from here?"

"There's an officer who will take you to your bungalow. You will be treated like royalty here. They have everything here. Best of luck to you both," he said as we were getting out of the chopper.

"Thanks, sergeant."

A lieutenant who escorted us to a waiting limo met us at the end of a walkway. It only took a couple of minutes for the limo to get us to our bungalow. We got out and walked up a path to the entrance and the lieutenant opened the door.

"It's all yours, Mr. and Mrs. Cannon, compliments of the FBI. Mr. Ferguson came by personally and made sure everything was in order. If you need anything at all, just pick up the red phone and I'll get you what you need," the officer said.

"Thank you very much, sir, but I'm sure everything will be fine," I said as he handed me another key.

"It's my pleasure," he said as he saluted, then turned and walked away.

As we walked in the door Gabriella began saying, "Jack, this is beautiful. Look at all these flowers."

"It looks like every person at the wedding sent some flowers."

"Jack, we even have champagne. There's a card here from Steve. It says, 'The best of the best for my friends. Good luck, Steve.' This is just too much," Gabriella said as tears began streaming down her cheeks.

"Gabriella, we really have some great friends, don't we?"

"The very best. I'll never forget this day as long as I live."

"Neither will I. Would you please come over here? I've got something I want to give you."

"I already know what it is, and I can hardly wait."

I noticed that look in her big brown eyes as she turned and walked to me. She put her arms around me, and we kissed for a very long time.

She pulled away slightly and said, "Give me just a minute while I go change into something I bought just for the occasion. I won't be gone but just a minute. I promise."

I watched as she took a small bag and went into the bathroom. She was so very beautiful. I still had a hard time believing all this had happened to me. I sat down on the edge of the bed and began to remove my clothes. I started thinking about the time we were going through one of our brief "I'm not going to see you anymore" episodes. They were very hard on us, but necessary at the time.

She had told me, "Jack, I'm very confused. I think we should stop seeing each other. I'm going to straighten everything out with Steve, and I can't do that and keep seeing you. You need someone that will treat you like you deserve to be treated" she said with a cold and distant look.

"Are you sure that's what you want?"

"Yes."

I remember that we talked for a few more minutes, but I really didn't know what to say. I felt my heart shattering. I finally just got up and walked away. It was unbearable. It lasted the longest three weeks of my life. I forgot who finally called whom, but it hurt us both.

"Jack, what are you thinking about?" Gabriella said as she came out of the bathroom.

She was wearing a pale-blue, baby-doll negligee that had nothing and everything. I had seen her many times, but I could never remember her looking more beautiful. She looked even more beautiful than the first time I had met her.

"It's not important. You look stunning. Come here to me now."

"Only if you tell me what you were thinking."

I knew she was serious so I said, "I was just thinking about one of the many times we tried to stop seeing each other. Remember the night at the restaurant when you said we had to stop?"

"Jack, I'm sorry. You know I had to try."

"I know. We sure hurt each other a lot back then, didn't we?"

"I was very confused then. I'm just glad you never gave up on me."

"Gabriella, as I told you then and I'll repeat now, we were meant to be together. I was sure then and I'm even more positive now. I love you."

"Jack, all of what has happened between us has been worth it. I'm going to make you so happy."

"You already have. Let's enjoy tonight."

I gently laid her on the bed beside me and started kissing her. She was soft and warm, and I couldn't believe that I'd be able to have her like this every night. What a sensation. As I kissed her neck, I moved slowly down her body. I stopped to caress both her breasts, not wanting to neglect either one. As I kissed each one of them, they became very hard. I moved down slowly and kissed every inch of her body that night. Just when I thought I would explode, Gabriella rolled me over and began kissing me. Slowly at first, then very passionately and intense. She started moving down my chest, and continued downward until it was evident that it was going to be like our night at the beach. We made love over and over again until we finally lay in each other's arms exhausted. She laid her head on my chest, and one leg draped across me as we kissed and fell fast asleep.

21

*T*HE PHONE IN THE BUNGALOW BEGAN RINGING, and I looked over at the clock. It was 3:00 P.M. in the afternoon. It felt as though we had just fallen asleep.

"Hello," I tried to say without much success.

"Jack, it's time to get up, ole buddy," I heard Gary say at the other end of the line.

"Man, I can't even hold my eyes open right now. What's the rush?"

"Well, there isn't any big rush, but all the families are here, and there's a big party that starts about six. You guys might want to be there. They have a big dinner planned for you and then dancing. It's a beautiful setup. Steve has it all arranged. Just call when you're ready. OK?"

"We'll be ready. I hope everyone is having a good time."

"Everything's fine, Jack. Everybody understands. This is your day, man. Enjoy it. We have to go to work soon enough."

"Yeah, I know. See you later," I said and hung up the phone.

I looked at Gabriella. She was facing away from me and had fallen asleep again. Her shoulder was showing, and I just lay there staring at her and watching her breath. She was so beautiful. After a few minutes, I slid over next to her, and put my arm around her to the front of her stomach. We fit together as if it was a form that had been made. I gently kissed her bare shoulder, and even more gently moved her hair out of the way so I could kiss her neck. I leaned down and just brushed my lips on her neck, not wanting to wake her. I then laid my head down on the pillow very close to her, expecting to sleep a while longer. I felt Gabriella's hand slide over to my hip, and she gripped me ever so softly. She then slid her hand down between my legs and began rubbing me. Almost before I realized it, she was facing me again. We made love and it was wonderful. How could it possibly be getting better? I love this woman.

It was after six when we had finally dressed, and I made the call to the lieutenant that we were ready. In a matter of seconds he was there with the limo. It took us only about two minutes to get to the main hotel building where everyone was waiting.

As the lieutenant escorted us from the limo to our destination inside the hotel, I couldn't help remembering how much both of our lives had changed and how much more life had in store for us. I prayed that the feelings between us would never end. One never knows exactly what life will bring to them, but we all must face it. The only thing that I was sure of was that God had sent this woman to me to be my soul mate. I had never been more certain of anything in my life.

"I planned this big party for you guys, at our expense, and you can't even get here on time. Is this the way it's going to be while you are working for me? What's up, anyway?" Steve said as we came through the doors of the hall that had been decorated for us.

"I begged Jack to get ready, but he wouldn't leave me alone. He's such a wild man now that he's able to walk again," Gabriella said joking around.

"I'll get you for that later. Steve, we both know that women are known for being late," I said as I put my arm around Gabriella and kissed her gently on the cheek.

"I'm just kidding. If it were me, I probably wouldn't be here at all."

"You'd be surprised how close you are to being right. It was very hard leaving our room," I said as we made our way to the front of the auditorium.

"This is the last of the festivities. After tonight, you guys have a couple of days to do whatever you want. It's on us. You just can't leave our little island," Steve said.

"Who would want too? It's beautiful here," Gabriella said.

"What happens after that, Steve?" I asked kind of matter of fact.

"Unfortunately, you guys have to go to work. I'll tell you all about it Thursday. Just enjoy the time you have. OK?"

"Thanks for everything, Steve. I hope we're able to do our job as well as you planned this out for us," Gabriella said.

"Don't worry. We'll have you ready and give you all the help you need."

Gabriella saw her parents and went over to talk to them while I went to speak with Connie and Kevin. The crying started all over again. It was all very touching, and I almost lost it myself a couple of times. Gabriella and I both knew that it might be quite a while before we saw any of our relatives again. We also knew that they would be instructed not to talk about this to anyone. We were working undercover and it was imperative that they must be quiet about the whole event. They would all cooperate, but it was going to be hard. This night had to be special and remembered.

We had a fantastic dinner that night, and even had a small band so that we could dance. The party went on until nearly 4:00 A.M., and we were all pretty drunk. Gary and I got up and sang a song or two with the band, and made complete fools of ourselves. It was great, but it had to come to an end. We would have to say good-bye to most of our relatives soon, and as we were leaving, all the women started hugging and crying all over again.

The next morning, after seeing everyone off, we spent the rest of the day in bed. We slept for a while, then made love until we were exhausted, and then slept again. Finally, at about 8:00 P.M., we showered together, dressed, and called the lieutenant so that we could go to dinner. We ate dinner quietly, and tried to get our strength back. It was wonderful. Gabriella still looked just as beautiful to me as she did when we first fell in love. That night we lay in bed and talked for a short while, and Gabriella fell asleep in my arms. It was the greatest feeling in the world.

The next day we went down to the beach and swam, sunned awhile, and went back to the bungalow and made love. It all ended too quickly for both of us. It was beginning to actually feel like we were growing together as one being.

22

THURSDAY MORNING WE WERE TO BE AT Steve's office at 9:00 A.M. When we entered the office, Cheryl and Gary were already there. Steve hadn't arrived yet.

"Good morning Mr. and Mrs. Cannon. How was your honeymoon?" Gary laughed and reached out to shake my hand.

"Not nearly long enough, but we'll take what we can get," Gabriella said.

"You guys even look married now. Some kind of glow or something," Cheryl added.

"Soulmates put on that glow, or didn't you know that?"

"That must be it," Cheryl said.

"Where's our leader?"

"No sign of him yet, anywhere. Something must have came up, because he's never late," Cheryl added.

"Well, I guess Jack and I can go back to the room for a while," Gabriella said with that devilish look in her eye.

"I don't think so," Gary quickly said.

"I'm sure he wouldn't mind," I said jokingly.

"Wouldn't mind what?" Steve said as he entered the door.

"Never mind," Gabriella quickly said and we all laughed.

"I guess it's one of those that I needed to be there for."

"I guess so," Gary answered.

"I hate to bring this all to an end, but we have a lot of things to cover this morning. Could you all be seated?" he said in a serious voice.

"I guess the honeymoon really is over."

"I'm afraid so, Jack. It's time to get serious about the job we have to do. Now, you guys are about as ready as time will allow, and things are getting worse in California. Gary. Cheryl. You two are leaving this weekend. Here are the addresses for your apartments. Cheryl, you start to work

Monday morning, and Gary, you start that following Friday. Classes start on the 26th of February, and that means everyone has to be in place by then. Any questions so far?"

"Steve, are Cheryl and I to know each other initially or later on?" Gary said.

"For the first couple of weeks, you guys will have no contact at all. After we get Jack and Gabriella in place, you guys can start dating."

"OK, but its going to be hard to stay away from this beautiful blonde for that long," Gary said as he put his arm around Cheryl.

"You'll survive. She's more woman than you can handle anyway," I said.

"Gentlemen," Steve said commanding our attention.

"Sorry, boss. Just kidding."

"Jack, you and Gabriella will fly into Dallas on the 20th and drive the rest of the way. Gabriella, we have arranged a job for you at a bank just off campus. It starts on that following Monday. Trucks from here will be taking out your furniture this week. All you two have to do is get one more week of training and then you're off. I know this is all coming together in a hurry, but we're forced to because of the university schedule. We'll meet again tomorrow morning to finalize everything. Today, the four of you will go over the details with one of the detectives who is already established out there. She will be your contact. Any questions now before I leave?"

"This person that we'll be working with today—does she work on campus?" Gary asked.

"No, but she is a student there. You'll find out more soon enough. Don't worry, everything has been arranged."

"Where do we meet her?" Cheryl asked.

"I told her to be in your office at 10:00 A.M. Her name is Sandy Nelson."

"OK, we'll be there," Cheryl said.

The rest of the day we spent with Sandy going over and over every detail of the setup. Sandy knew all the guys we were after, and we discussed them thoroughly. I have the pleasure of working with another attractive woman. She was Hispanic, with very long black curly hair, big beautiful eyes and she was stunning. She and Gabriella hit it off immediately. They started talking in Spanish and left us all out.

By the end of the day we were worn out. We left the building at about 6:00 P.M., grabbed a quick dinner, and headed back to the hotel for sleep. I was very tired, and could tell that it would be a while before I had all my strength back. That night Gabriella and I fell asleep in each other's arms. What a way to end the day.

The next day we again reviewed every detail of the mission. Sandy would tell us about this or that, and then we would all ask questions. She kept reminding us how important it was to have every detail down perfectly. She also reminded us that all the other efforts that the agency had made had failed. We knew it would be difficult to make this all work.

That same afternoon we knocked off about 4:00 and met Steve at one of the local restaurants. This was to be our farewell dinner together.

"Here's a toast to our success," Steve said as we all lifted our glasses.

"And here's a toast to the person who got us all in this mess," I said and we all laughed.

"Tomorrow it all starts for real. Do you guys have any questions about what we're going to do?"

"Steve, do we have some kind of code name for what we are about to do? I don't mean to sound like a movie, but we're all new at this, and I was just curious," Gabriella said kind of shyly.

"I'm glad you asked. We hadn't picked out anything in particular because we were going to let the five of you decide. Any ideas?"

"I have an idea. It may sound a little dumb, but I thought that since we've all become such close friends why not call it 'Friends'?" Gabriella asked.

"That doesn't sound so dumb to me. We have all become close friends. I think 'Friends' it should be," Cheryl said.

"You don't think for one minute that I'm going to argue with either of them, do you?" Gary said.

"I know I'm not," I said.

"That just leaves you, Sandy," Steve said.

"Hey, don't look at me. I'm the newest member of this crazy bunch. I'll tell you one thing. You guys are great together, and I'm glad I get to work with you."

"Well, that settles it, then. I guess 'good friends' are going to put an end to our problems in California," Steve stated.

"I think a toast is in order. To good friends," Gary said.

We all took a big swig of our drinks to toast our new assignment. After that we had dinner and talked for a while. After a few hours, we all went our separate ways. I think everyone was anxious to get started. It was new and exciting, and still very scary. None of us really knew just what to expect. Gary and Cheryl still had some packing to do and were the first to leave. Next, Steve excused himself.

"I'll see you guys in the morning. Sandy, don't keep them out too late."

"No problem, boss. I have an early flight. Besides, our newlyweds might want to get home early."

"We're just going to finish our drinks, and we're going to our room too. Gabriella and I have a little business to take care of," I said smiling.

"Right!" Steve said smiling back.

23

*T*HAT NEXT MORNING SANDY, CHERYL, AND GARY met us at the office. They had separate flights, and were gone by noon. We continued our training the rest of the day. Friday, we were ready to fly to Dallas, and then drive the rest of the way. Our background was set up to be from Dallas, and our car would be waiting there.

"Jack, take care of that beautiful wife of yours. It would be hard to find anyone like her anywhere. Oh yeah, you be careful, too," Steve said while patting me on the back and laughing as we were walking through the airport.

"Don't worry about us, Steve. You taught us well. Besides that, you said everything was taken care of. All we have to do is get you some evidence. Right?" I said, half smiling.

"Just be careful, my friend. I want you guys back here by Memorial Day."

"We'll try our best, Steve," Gabriella said.

"I know you will. We're going to get them this time. Here's your gate. We only have a couple of minutes before you guys have to board."

"Thanks for all you've done for us, Steve."

"No. Thank you."

In a matter of minutes we were on the plane and in the air. We arrived in Dallas at 3:00 P.M. and one of the agents was there to get us to our car. We soon headed west from Dallas and drove until early evening. After a quick dinner, we continued driving until almost midnight. By Sunday night, we had finally reached our destination—the beautiful university town of San Diego. The school was at least one hundred years old, and most of the town and surrounding area must have been built about the same time as the university. There were signs of modernization with malls and night-clubs, but for the most part, older buildings surrounded the school. We rode around for a while just looking and getting familiar with the town. It was beautiful and it seemed so quiet. It was kind of a surprise that so much drug dealing was going on in this setting. It wasn't hard to figure out where the people with all the money lived. On the west end of town, there was a subdivision that had houses that were worth well over a million apiece. This must be where Willie Hernandez lived.

"Jack, wouldn't it be nice if we lived in one of the houses out here?"

"I'm sure Steve put us in a nice house, but I doubt they'd put out that kind of money on a house like that."

We drove back downtown and went to a 7-11 to get directions to our house.

"Could you tell me where Randall Street is?"

"It's in that new subdivision out west of town. Go back down Broad and follow it to the entrance to Errol Estates. Then you can just ask the security guard exactly where it is," the clerk said.

"Are you sure that's where it is?"

"No other Randall Street in this town."

"Thanks, my friend."

"No problem," he said as I headed back to the car.

"I hope we're close to the house. I'm getting really tired," Gabriella said.

"It's not too far away. I think you might be a little surprised."

"Did we drive right by it?"

"We were pretty close."

"Jack, we just came down this road."

"I know, honey. We're going back where we just came from."

"Not in there."

"Yes, in there."

"Are you sure?"

"Just calm down and we'll see what Steve has in store for us."

I pulled up to the entrance, and a security guard came out of a small, air-conditioned building.

"May I help you?" he said.

"Yes, I'm looking for 1130 Randall Street. Is it in here?"

"It sure is. Can I have your name please, and I'll call ahead to let them know you're here."

"Well, my name is Cannon, Jack Cannon, but you can't call ahead. We're the new owners."

"OK, Mr. Cannon, just let me check and I'll be right back," the guard said as he went back inside the guardhouse.

After a few seconds he came back out and said, "Welcome to Errol Estates, Mr. Cannon. Your house is in the new section in the back. Just go down to the end of this street, take a right, and it is the last house on the right. If you have any problems, just give me a call. Here's my number and the code to your security system. I just need to see your driver's license to verify who you are."

"No problem," I said as I showed him my new Texas driver's license.

"You're all set, Mr. and Mrs. Cannon. Don't hesitate to call if you have any questions."

"Thank you," I said as we drove off.

"Well, Gabriella, this is it," I said as we pulled into the driveway of a brand-new home at the end of the street.

"Jack, it's so big and beautiful. I can't wait to see the inside."

"It must be worth at least a million dollars, Gabriella. I can't believe Steve put us here. I guess we have to look the part. Are you ready?"

"Let's go."

After I entered the security code and unlocked the door, I turned to Gabriella, who was behind me smiling, "Come here, Mrs. Cannon. I want to give you a big kiss."

She walked to me, and put her arms around me and kissed me. As we finished, I leaned down and picked her up. I pushed the door and walked in. Once we were inside, we couldn't believe what we were seeing. It was even more beautiful than we had imagined it would be.

"Jack, I can't believe this. It's so big."

"I know. Where do you want to start, left or right?"

"Left."

We were standing in a large foyer. Straight ahead, we could see an entrance to what looked like the kitchen. We started left and found three large bedrooms. Two of them had a connecting bathroom. The other had a separate bathroom with two large walk-in closets. We both assumed this must be the master bedroom. All three rooms were completely furnished. After walking through all three bedrooms, we headed back to where the kitchen was and entered the door. It was huge—kind of oval. Along the wall was the refrigerator, oven, microwave, sinks, and cabinets. In the middle was the stove with a large counter and bar stools. Above it hung every pot and pan that you could imagine. On the other side was a large booth that would seat six people. Next to that was a large walk-in pantry full of food.

"Gabriella, we could live in this kitchen."

"I can't believe this. It's so big. Oh, Jack, look out the window. We have a pool. Come here."

"Guess what we're going to do in that pool," I said as I stood there with my arms around her.

"I can hardly wait. Let's see the rest."

We walked out the other side of the kitchen and saw a very large living room. It had a freestanding fireplace in the middle with couches all around. Built into the wall was a complete home entertainment center with the largest big screen TV I had ever seen. It must have been five feet by five feet. There were over-stuffed couches all around it. All of this was to the left. To the right was a huge dining room with a table that seated twelve people.

"Gabriella, I hope we meet some people soon or we're going to have to waste a beautiful dining room."

"We'll have to have an intercom to talk to one another. Steve really is going to spoil us. I'm not sure I'm going to want to give this up," Gabriella said smiling.

"Gabriella, you're not going to believe this," I said as I passed through double doors and saw what turned out to be the master bedroom. It was as large as the living room. In the center of the room was another freestanding fireplace. One entire glass wall faced the pool. As we walked through another door, we saw a huge oval tub.

Next to it was an even larger hot tub. To the left of the room, there were two large walk-in closets and they were full of clothes.

"Jack, look at these clothes. They must have cost a fortune," Gabriella said as she browsed through the closet that was full of stuff for her.

"That's the way they do it, Gabriella. We move in and everything is set up. We do have to look the part. Remember?"

"I know, Jack, but I wasn't expecting this."

"Why don't we try out the hot tub. We need to make sure it works right?" I said, and she knew exactly what I meant.

"I'll bet I can get there first," she said as she began taking off her clothes.

24

O N MONDAY MORNING, EVERYTHING STARTED for real. Gabriella reported to her job at the bank, and I went to the campus for my first day of work.

"I'm here to see Mr. Lawrence. My name is Jack Cannon. I think he is expecting me," I told the secretary.

"Oh yes, Mr. Cannon. Mr. Lawrence is expecting you. Just have a seat, and I'll let him know you're here," the secretary said. She turned and entered an office behind her. After a few minutes she returned and said, "He'll see you now, Mr. Cannon. Right this way."

I entered the office, and saw Mr. Lawrence sitting behind a large oak desk in a huge cushioned chair that almost swallowed him. He didn't look like your typical university president. He was in his mid-thirties and had long, black, curly hair that touched the back of his neck. He was smoking a small-tipped cigar while he looked over some papers as I crossed the room.

"Mr. Cannon, please have a seat, and I'll be right with you."

He continued looking over more papers and signing this and that. Finally, he stood and extended his hand for me to shake.

"Mr. Cannon, it's nice to finally meet you. I've heard a lot of good things about you. How's your novel coming?"

"Fine, thank you. It's nice to meet you, too, Mr. Lawrence."

"Please call me Matt. I'm not a big stickler on last names. I hope you don't mind if I call you Jack."

"Not at all."

"Good. Now, I've seen tapes of these introductory classes you do and I'd like for you do a couple of them here."

"No problem, I enjoy those the best. What else?"

"Two accounting classes and a marketing class. You'll need to get with Daniel Berkley sometime today and get your text. Classes start on Wednesday so that doesn't leave you much time."

"Sounds great to me. How do I find Daniel?"

"If you don't mind, check with my secretary and she'll get you to him. I have a million things going on today. Let's get together for lunch one day this week."

"Just let me know when. Thanks again," I said as I shook his hand.

His secretary gave me a map of the campus, and made an **X** on the appropriate area for the College of Accounting. Of course it was at the far end of the campus, but I enjoyed the walk. The campus was beautiful. All the buildings were very old, but well kept, with wide sidewalks and green grass all around. Palm trees were scattered all over the campus grounds. Students were camped out everywhere, either studying, playing, or just talking. I finally found the College of Accounting. I entered the building, and asked one of the students who was working there for directions to Mr. Berkley's office. As she turned around I was surprised to see Sandy standing there. "Mr. Berkley's office is down the hall to your left. Room 127. If I can help anymore just stop by."

"Thank you, ma'am."

"You're welcome," she said and smiled as I turned and walked away. The agency had thought of everything. I hadn't expected to see Sandy working there. That would help a great deal.

I knocked on the door at room 127 and heard someone holler, "Come in." When I opened the door and entered, the first thing I saw were books everywhere. There was a man sitting behind a desk that was also full of books. He was smoking a pipe and reading something. He looked to be in his late thirties and had a small earring in his left ear.

"Have a seat Cannon. I'll be with you in a minute. Just set those books on the floor," he said without looking up.

"Thank you, Mr. Berkley."

"Just call me Dan."

"OK, Dan."

After a few minutes, he looked up from what he was doing and said, "Jack, I have two accounting books, a marketing text, and a college-success book ready for you on the table. Can you have me a syllabi ready for the class by noon tomorrow?"

"That shouldn't be any problem. Do you have a class schedule, and some old syllabi that I can use as a guide?"

He stood and walks to a file cabinet behind him, fumbled around for a couple of minutes and then handed them to me. "These should help you out. Your office is down the hall. Room 145. I'm afraid you'll have to share it with three other professors. I hope that's not a problem."

"Not at all, Dan. I'll have this ready for you as soon as I can."

"The girl at the information desk out front can help you get copies made and answer any questions you have if you can't find me."

"Thanks, Dan, I'll talk to you later."

I found my office, and spent the next couple of hours working on my course outlines. About noon I left the office and went to the information desk.

"Excuse me, can you tell me where I can get something to eat?"

"Sure Professor Cannon, go out the door and to the left two buildings. There's a cafeteria on the second floor. By the way, my name is Sandy. If you need anything else just give me a holler."

"Thank you, Sandy. I'll probably have a million questions."

"I'll answer as many as I can."

"OK. See you later."

I left the campus about 4:00 P.M. so I could get to the bank and pick up Gabriella.

"How was your first day, beautiful lady," I said after giving her a kiss when she got in the car.

"Great. How about yours?"

"It felt good to be back on campus. Any campus. The place is beautiful. You'll have to come and see it."

"OK, I'll come by. I want to make sure you're behaving yourself."

"Please do. You'll never know," I said smiling at her.

"Oh yes, I know. I love you, Jack."

"I love you too."

During the next several weeks, we began to get into our work duties. Classes had started, and I was getting to know some of the students. Gabriella was enjoying her job at the bank, and we were starting to act like a family. It was a shame that all this wouldn't last very long. But we were both aware of the job we had to do and there were a couple of things that still needed to be done. One was to meet this guy Willie, and another to get in good with one of the students at school so that I could start buying drugs. The latter would be easy, because of all the contact I have with them. It's always easy to spot somebody who uses. The hard part would be meeting Willie. I couldn't think of any good ways yet, so I decided to wait and ask Sandy for suggestions.

Gabriella and I had began walking around the neighborhood every evening for exercise and to get a look at Willie's house. We would always see a few cars parked out front. The house was like some of the very expensive houses that I use to see in South Florida. All across the front entrance were large columns that were about three-foot round, and probably twenty-foot high. There was a balcony across the second story of the house. The walkway had about ten stairs leading up to the front doors that were fifteen-feet tall and at least eight-feet wide. Each window had iron bars, and the doors had bars that could be closed at night. The limo and the black Jaguar were in the driveway every evening we passed. We could hear music being played in one of the upstairs rooms. The house and all the trim were painted white, and the iron bars were all in pink.

We caught a glimpse of Willie one evening, and he waved as he passed in his Jag. We were into our third week of walks around the neighborhood when the Jag slowed next to us. We were right near Willie's house.

"It doesn't look to me like either of you guys need exercise," the voice from the car said.

"It's really just a way of winding down after a long day at work, but the exercise doesn't hurt."

"You ought to come try out my gym sometime. It would probably be fun, and my fitness guy could give you some suggestions about equipment that could release that tension. By the way, my name is Willie Hernandez, and I live in that house right over there," he said pointing down the road.

"It's nice to meet you, Mr. Hernandez, I'm...."

"You're Jack Cannon, and this must be your lovely wife, Gabriella. Right?"

"Yes, but how did you know? We just moved here less than a month ago."

"Well, this is a small town, and I try to keep up with what's going on."

"To be honest with you, Mr. Hernandez, we thought you were the chauffeur," Gabriella added with a smile.

"Please call me Willie, Mrs. Cannon. All my friends do, and I insist that you and your husband become my friends as of this moment. I can't have you keep thinking I'm the driver," he said smiling and staring at Gabriella.

"Thank you, Willie. You'll have to call us Gabriella and Jack. That way we just eliminated a lot of unnecessary formality. We just love your home. Did you design it yourself?" Gabriella asked.

"Yes I did. Would you like to see the inside of it sometime?"

"If you don't mind. I use to be in the construction business, and I always like to look at the interiors of new homes to see what other people can come up with."

"I'm sure you'll like this one. I sank a lot of money into every detail. Why don't you stop by tomorrow night about this time and I'll give you the tour?"

"I wish we could, but I'm working late tomorrow evening grading papers. How about the night after," I said not wanting to seem too anxious.

"Sure, why not. You teach at the university, right? Small town, remember. Got to run. See you guys later," and he gunned the car and was gone. He pulled in the driveway, and before he could turn off the engine, his chauffeur was there to open the door of the Jag. As he exited the car, he turned and waved at us. We returned the wave.

And just like that, we had meet Willie Hernandez. He seemed to be just the way we had studied and learned about him. I decided not to go to his house as invited. We'd just wait and see what happened. I wanted to make sure he knew that we weren't in any rush to get chummy.

About a week later, Gabriella and I were taking our usual walk around the neighborhood, and were almost back to the house when that same Jag approached us. I was sure it was Willie about to ask us why we hadn't been to his house.

"Excuse me, Mr. Cannon, Mrs. Cannon. Willie asked me to check with you and see if you had a minute to stop by his home," the man inside the car said.

"I'm sure we could drop over later. What do you think, Jack?"

"Please tell Mr. Hernandez that we'll stop by in about fifteen minutes."

This guy was very big. Maybe six-five, 290 pounds. He had to be Spanish because of his dark complexion and heavy accent. He opened the car door and kind of stood there half in and half out of the car, and turned to us again and stated, "Willie said I should follow you home and wait for you. I hope you don't mind, sir."

"Not at all. We just live right over there," I said pointing at our house.

"Yes sir, I know. My name is José, and if it's OK with you, I'll give you a lift and wait while you get ready."

"No. No. That will be fine. It will only take us a minute."

A smile came to his face as I said that, and he quickly came around to the other side of the Jag and opened the door for us. "Here you are, Mrs. Cannon. Mr. Cannon. Just jump right in."

It seemed like the guy was happy just accomplishing this small feat for his boss. He was smiling like a schoolboy who had just made the baseball team. It's probably the hardest task he had all day. He again opened the door as we arrived at our house.

"I guess Willie really wants to see us," Gabriella said when we were inside.

"Maybe he really just wants to see you," I said jokingly to Gabriella. She took a playful swing at me.

"Well just maybe, he wants to have you near him," she said, continuing our little joke.

"You could be right," I stated in my best feminine voice.

In a matter of minutes, we were back in the Jag and pulling in the driveway of Willie's house or should I say, castle. As we came to a stop, José again jumped out of the car and opened the door. We began our walk up the steps.

"I figured this was the only sure way of getting you guys over here. I don't like being stood up. Good job, José," he said all in one breath as he came walking out of the "castle."

"We didn't mean to stand you up, Willie. Jack and I...."

"Hey, I was just kidding. I just wanted to make sure you came by before I had to go out of the country. Besides, Jose bet me he could get you over here."

"He was very convincing, and big enough that I wasn't going to turn him down," I said, half laughing but meaning every word of it.

"Well, come on in and let me show you around my modest living quarters. I sank a lot of money in this place and I'm always happy to show it off."

"Willie, you really can't tell it's this big from the outside," Gabriella said as we entered the front door.

"Well just follow me, and I'll give you the five-dollar tour. Would you care for something to drink?"

"I'll have a White Russian, if you don't mind."

"How about you, Gabriella?"

"Just a Pepsi, if it's not too much trouble."

"Not at all. One moment please while I call my friend to make them. Maria," he shouted.

"Yeah, Willie. What you want," a woman shouted back as she came walking in from another room.

"Maria. Say hello to Gabriella and Jack Cannon. They live just down the road."

"Very pleased to meet you. Sorry I shouted. I didn't realize we had company. Why didn't you tell me you were inviting someone over, Willie? I would have cleaned up a little."

"You look great, baby. Don't you think so, Jack?"

"Definitely!"

"Maria, you look fine! Glad to meet you," piped Gabriella.

"See. I told you so. Would you get a White Russian for Jack, and a Pepsi for Gabriella, and bring them upstairs."

"No problem. I'll be up in a minute."

Maria was a very attractive brunette, with dark brown eyes. She had very high cheekbones, and even though she appeared Hispanic, I thought she might have Indian blood in her. She was definitely attractive. She was one of those women that could wear Spandex and look really good. She was average height and weight, but that was all that was average about her. Of course, I wouldn't expect anything less from Willie knowing what I do about him. He is known to have a weakness for beautiful women. Then again, don't all men?

Willie directed us to the stairway on the right side of the hall, which lead to a sunken living room. It wrapped around in an oval leading to the second story of the castle. There was a matching stairway on the other side. At the top of the stairs, we made a right turn and were escorted through eight bedrooms that were all at least twenty feet by thirty feet. Each one was decorated in a different Spanish decor and had its own bath. And of course, each had its own balcony facing either to the front or rear of the castle. From there we made our way to the other side of the castle that turned out to be where Willie had his bedroom, exercise room, bathroom, and theater (with a twelve-foot by twenty-foot screen and real movie-style chairs). His bedroom took up the entire left side of the house. It was also done in Spanish decor, and had pictures everywhere that he described as "his investments in the future." There was a sunken, free-standing fireplace in the center of the bedroom, with oversize cushions all around it. Every room in the house was done in dark colors such as black, brown, dark gray, and even dark green. It sounds terrible, but everything seem to match perfectly. He told us that he had a processional designer fly in to decorate the house. An old friend or something.

By the time we made our way downstairs, we had already finished our drinks and Maria met us at the bottom of the stairs with another. We continued down the large hall to a room that sank into a huge formal living room. I say formal, because I doubt that anyone spent much time in there. Everything looked very expensive and unused. The kitchen had all the stuff that a restaurant would ever need. An older woman Willie called "Mom" was cooking over one of the stoves. We didn't slow down for introductions, because Willie had explained she wasn't really his mom, just the cook. The dining room was equipped to feed a small army. The table had twelve chairs on each side and one on each end.

We walked out the sliding glass doors at the back of the house, which lead to a large covered patio. He pointed to the riding stables on the left, the tennis and basketball court straight ahead, and the Olympic-size swimming pool to the right.

"Why don't we have a seat over here," he said as he pulled out a chair for Gabriella and directed us to sit down. "What do you think of my little treasure?"

"Willie, it's just beautiful. Your decorator did a wonderful job with all the color schemes," Gabriella said almost in amazement.

"I have to say I'm really impressed. I can understand if you never leave the house. You have everything."

"Yeah, almost everything. Sometimes I just get tired of it, and have to fly away for a few days."

We sat and talked for about thirty minutes, and then all of sudden it seemed as though Willie might be getting bored. "I hate to seem like I'm trying to run you guys off, but I have a very important business meeting at seven-thirty. I haven't even started getting ready yet. You're welcome to stay as long as you want, but I must excuse myself. José will drive you home when you're ready."

"We understand, Willie. It's getting late, and I still have papers to grade anyway. Thank you for the tour of the house."

Gabriella smiled. "You will have to come and have dinner with us very soon. I promise I'm really a good cook."

"Thank you guys for coming over, and call me when you want me for dinner," he said as he was turning around to leave the patio. "José take the Cannons home whenever they are ready."

"Sure thing, Willie. Mr. Cannon, just let me know when."

"We're ready now, if you don't mind, José."

"Please follow me this way, and I'll take you to the car."

25

M*R. CANNON, DO YOU ALWAYS* invite your students out for drinks after class like this," a student named Andy Marks asked me as we sat at the bar having a drink.

"Andy, I think I said I was coming here to have a drink, and you just happened to be here."

"Right, Mr. Cannon."

"Listen, I can get in trouble asking students out for drinks, no matter how innocent it is. That's why I always just say where I'm going. Understand?" I whispered to him

"I understand. I was just curious."

"I like to hang out with my students because I feel I can learn a lot from them, too. Besides, we're all just people."

"Not many professors feel that way. They think we are below them or something."

"I don't think that's it. It has something to do with image. They think they have to set themselves apart."

"Why don't you?"

"I always enjoyed professors who could relate. This is part of the way I do that. By this time next semester you'll see that my classes are always full. I'm very good at what I do, so I must be doing something right." I could tell that he was buying every word I said. This was almost too easy.

"I can't believe how you make everyone in the class get loose so quick."

"People just want to be treated like people. Anyway, let's forget all this stuff and have another drink."

"Sounds good to me."

We had a couple of more drinks and talked about school, sports, women, and eventually about drugs. Now came the real test.

"So, Andy, do you party, man?"

"Um...sometimes."

"Well, let's ease out to my car and fire one up."

When he finally left that afternoon, not only was he stoned, he was convinced that I was the coolest professor to ever hit California. The stage was being set.

During the next few weeks, Andy and I met at the bar and had drinks. We always managed to get to my car and get high. One day he would furnish the pot, and the next I'd furnish it. I always managed to let him know that his was much better than mine was.

"I brought this stuff with me from where I use to live. Not bad, huh?"

"Pretty good, but I think the stuff I have is better," he said as we sat in my car again.

"Well, I only have a little left, and then I have to start looking for another source."

"No problem at all man. I can pick you up some."

"That's great. I'll let you know."

* * *

"Honey, I'm making great progress with Andy. I'll start buying from him next week. Sandy said that we should all get together this weekend. How about a little housewarming party?" I said as we were driving home.

"That sounds great, Jack. Can we invite lots of people? I can get Cheryl to help. I can decorate the house a little. Can we do it Saturday night?"

"Hey, slow down. We have to check it out with Sandy. I don't think she will mind, though. We'll invite Willie and his buddies too. Kind of mix business with pleasure."

"We could have a great party. I can hardly wait. Do you think that everyone will be able to tell how very much I love you?" She said smiling and leaning over to give me a kiss. She put her arms around me, and laid her head on my shoulder. At times she was like a little kid, and other times she was older than I was. I loved both sides of her.

"I'm sure by the time the night is over, everyone will be able to tell how much in love we are."

"I'll call Cheryl tomorrow and tell her to invite Gary. Don't forget to call Sandy," she said as she looked up at me with those big brown eyes. They still have the same effect on me that they had the very first time we met. I couldn't believe one man could be so happy.

I called Sandy the next morning from a pay phone. "How about us having a housewarming party Saturday night. I could invite Willie and his crowd, the president of the university, Gary, Cheryl, and that student from school, Andy."

"That sounds great, Jack. We could all get together and talk for awhile before the party, and also make some contacts with Willie's people. Just make sure you invite enough people from all the different areas so that it looks normal."

"No problem, Sandy. Be sure and bring a date. You do know someone that you can bring, don't you?" I said laughing.

"You just take care of your end. I have lots of guys who'd kill to go out with me."

"I knew that. Talk to you later."

When I got to the campus I called Gabriella and told her to get started planning. She was so excited she could hardly talk. This was the first party we had given since we were married. During the day I managed to invite Matt, Dan, Andy, and a couple of students from each of my classes.

"Let me guess how many people you've already invited," I said to Gabriella that night when we got home.

"Not really that many, Jack. Cheryl and Gary, some people from work, and our neighbors. Did you call Willie?"

"Not yet. How about handing me the phone and I'll do it now."

She grabbed the phone off the end table and handed it towards me. "After I get a kiss and then only if you are a good boy." She had that look.

After making love to her for a couple of hours, I called Willie. "Could I speak to Willie Hernandez? This is Jack Cannon."

"What was the name, man," the voice at the other end said.

"Jack Cannon."

"Hold on a minute."

I held on what seemed like forever, but finally I heard Willie say, "Jack, how you doing, man?"

"Just fine, Willie. I almost hung up. I thought whoever answered the phone forgot I was here."

"Nah. I was out back cooking some steaks on the grill. Sorry about that. How's the teaching business? You get rich or what, my friend?"

"If I didn't have money before I started teaching, I'd be broke by now. I do a lot of investing."

"So do I, man. Lots of investing."

"We need to sit and talk about that somctime. By the way, how about you and some of your friends coming over Saturday night for a little house-warming party."

"All you had to was mention party. I'm in. I was going to stay in Mexico over the weekend, but I'll be back for your party. What time, man?"

"Say around eight o'clock. That's all right for you?"

"Sure man, how many people can I bring? I have lots of friends."

"It doesn't matter as long as I know about how many so I can have enough food and stuff."

"Not many. Maybe ten or so. Is that all right?"

"Sure, Willie."

"OK. Yeah man. I'll bring the booze and stuff. You just get the food."

"You don't have to do that."

"Yeah, I know, but it's the least I can do. Got to run, man. See you Saturday night."

"Goodnight."

"Later, dude," and he hung up.

"All set, Gabriella, and he's bringing the booze."

26

I WOKE UP EARLY SATURDAY MORNING and rolled over with my eyes still closed, expecting to feel this warm body next to me, but there was no body. We usually made love before we even got out of bed, took showers together, and then dressed and went out for breakfast. That was our special Saturday morning treat that was made more exciting by the fact that we were always trying to see who would wake up first, and come up with something different to start the activities. She was becoming better and better at it, and I missed her not being there when I woke up.

I reluctantly got out of bed and went looking for her. The house was quiet, but I heard music coming from out in the backyard. As I walk out on the back porch, I saw her standing on top of a ladder. She was hanging some lights for the party. Her hair was in a ponytail and she was wearing very tight shorts and a T-shirt. As she was leaning to hang them, she kind of wiggled around, and it was driving me crazy. I just stood there and watched as she worked. She was stunning.

She climbed down off the ladder and turned her head. "How long have you been standing there, Mr. Cannon," she smiled.

"Long enough to come over and grab you, pick you up, and carry you back to bed, Mrs. Cannon."

"Jack, we don't have time for that this morning if you want us to be ready for the party. Don't look at me that way," she said.

"I just want a little hug and kiss, and then I'll help you."

"Oh sure. I know that look. It always starts out with a little hug and kiss. Good morning, darling," and she put her arms around me, and kiss me gently knowing that anything more would be fatal.

"Good morning, beautiful lady. I missed waking up next to you."

"I knew if I woke you up, we'd never get ready for the party. Just remember this Jack, you're everything in my life and I love you," and she kissed me again.

"If you kiss me one more time...."

"I promise to make it up to you tonight after the party. We'll make love until dawn. I promise."

"Deal," I said as my mind began to wonder off in thoughts of things that would happen that night.

The rest of the morning and part of the afternoon we arranged things for the party.

At about four o'clock, Cheryl and Gary arrived. About half an hour later Sandy showed up. We talked about what we were trying to accomplish at the party, while we continued to decorate and get things ready.

"Jack, I want you and Gabriella to get as close to Willie as you can tonight. Hang with him as much as possible. Just be careful. This guy is very cautious," Sandy said.

"No problem, Sandy. We'll be careful."

"Gary, Cheryl, and I will kind of mingle. We can't let him or any of his people get suspicious. I think we can get to know them tonight, and maybe set up things for another time."

"What if Willie or one of his people bring up the subject of drugs," Gary asked.

"I'd avoid any direct answer. If they ask you about getting high or something, you handle that carefully. They may be just testing you. For tonight, we just want to gather information and have a good time."

As we continued to talk, a big truck pulled up in the driveway. It was unmarked except for licensing numbers on the doors. Two men got out and came to the door.

"Is this the Cannon residence," one of the men asked.

"I'm Jack Cannon."

"We have a delivery for you. Where do you want us to put it."

"What is it you're delivering?"

"Let me see," the other guy said as he looked at some papers he had on a clipboard. "Five cases of Corona, five cases of Michelob Light, ten cases of various kinds of liquor, and five cases of wine. Oh yeah, and a case of champagne."

"Willie Hernandez sent all that here," I kind of stated and asked at the same time.

"Yeah, that's the guy who's paying the bill," the driver said.

"Well, I guess you'd better put it out on the back porch for now. I'll have to get some ice and something to put it in first."

"That's all taken care of, Mr. Cannon. We brought everything you'll need. Mr. Hernandez made sure of that."

"Well then, have a beer on Mr. Hernandez as you unload it."

"Thanks, Mr. Cannon. As soon as we get it set up we'll take you up on that. Just lead the way."

I turned and lead them around the side of the house, and showed them where to put the stuff.

"He must plan on having a party for the whole town," Gary said.

"If everybody drinks all this, we should end up with enough information to put us all in jail for life," Sandy continued.

"Let's remember not to get carried away," Gabriella added.

"Everyone will do fine. Cheryl, do you and Gary know who you are going to have your contact with?" Sandy asked.

"Yeah, we'll hang with Matt and the other faculty."

"The rest we'll just play by ear," Sandy said.

"Where's your date, Sandy?" Gabriella asked.

"I told him to be here about seven. You guys know Kevin McMullen. He's in law school. Pretty nice guy."

"How nice is he?" Gabriella said smiling as she, Cheryl, and Sandy headed out back to do some more work.

"I don't know him that well yet, but I will."

Gary and I made sure we had plenty of glasses and cups set up outside. It was almost time for everyone to start arriving.

Sandy's date arrived on time and from then on everyone started to trickle in. By eight o'clock, all our guests had arrived except Willie and all his people. I had plenty of music loaded on the stereo, and everybody was starting to get to know each other when we heard a loud commotion at the front of the house. I went to the front door and couldn't believe my eyes. There was a limo, three Mercedes, three Bemers, and another panel truck stopped out front.

Willie was first out of the limo and hollered, "Jack, sorry we're late, but my plane just got in a few minutes ago. I hope you don't mind, but I brought a band along. Can't have a party with out proper music. Most of them are relatives of mine from Mexico. I mentioned party and they had to come along."

"Not at all, Willie. Why should I complain? Besides, we have enough booze for all of Southern California, thanks to you."

"I just wanted to make sure we had enough. We can always use what's left for the next party. Now, where's that beautiful wife of yours," he said already heading towards the back of the house.

"You're headed in the right direction."

"OK. My friends, just follow me. Jack, I'll introduce everyone as soon as I get the band going."

He must have brought twenty-five people with him, if you count the band. I recognized some of the guys and few of the women from our previous visits to his house. They all looked like money people.

There was a very stunning woman that Willie kept very close to him that I hadn't seen before. She had long black hair and dark eyes. She was wearing a bulky pink sweater and very tight jeans that looked as if someone had made them just to fit her. This was star quality. She didn't look Spanish or Italian, but she did have a dark, rich tan, and I was sure she had no tan lines anywhere. As the old saying goes, "she looked familiar, but I couldn't place her." I had probably seen her in a magazine or something. As she passed by me, she looked at me for a few seconds and I kind of sensed something. It wasn't a look of two people attracted to each other, but a curious look. I had the feeling that she might have thought she knew me too.

Willie took charge of the place when he got to our back yard. Speaking in Spanish, he began to tell all the people what and where to go. It wasn't long before the band began to play and everyone was being fed. One of the guys that came with Willie became the bartender and another went around making sure everyone had a full drink.

"Jack, Willie sure brought a lot of people with him," Gabriella said as she joined me out by the pool.

"I count twenty-five."

"I guess he likes to make sure that there really is a party when he comes. I haven't seen that girl with him before, have you?"

"No. She must be his main woman. Very beautiful though, wouldn't you agree?"

"Put your tongue back in your mouth. You're taken, remember!"

"Absolutely. She doesn't come close to you darling," I said as I leaned and kissed her very softly. "No one comes close to you."

"You were staring at her, Jack."

"She just looks familiar, that's all. You're not jealous, are you?"

"Any woman that can make you stare like that, makes me jealous."

"Never, ever, worry about anyone. I'm yours forever. Soulmates remember?"

"I love you, my soulmate."

"I love you, too, beautiful lady."

"Shall we go meet them?"

"You lead the way."

As we walked off, she pinched me on the behind and started to laugh. I grabbed her and put my arm around her waist as we continued toward Willie.

"Jack, my man, great party. The place looks great. I hope we don't run out of booze," Willie said as we approached.

"I don't think there's any chance at all that we'll run out of anything, thanks to you. It really is turning out to be a great party."

"Let me introduce you and Gabriella to my friends." He said as he started telling us everyone's name. He seemed to be saving the woman for last. We shook hands with everyone as he continued.

"Now let me introduce you to my very special friend. Jack and Gabriella, this is Michelle Duncan. Michelle, this is Jack and Gabriella Cannon. He's the professor at the university I was telling you about."

"Nice to meet you, Miss Duncan," I said as she extended her hand and I shook it gently.

"It's nice to meet you, too, but please call me Michelle. It's nice to meet you too, Mrs. Cannon."

"Please call me, Gabriella. It's a pleasure to meet you."

"I met Michelle in L.A. a couple of years ago, and we've been friends ever since," Willie said.

"That's a beautiful sweater you have on Michelle. Did you get it in L.A.?" Gabriella said.

"Actually, I bought it in a little shop just outside of Reno last week. It was a steal. Gabriella, could you show me wherethe little girl's room is?"

"Just follow me, I need to check my makeup anyway," Gabriella added, as they joined hands like little kids and headed for the bathroom.

"She's very beautiful, Willie. I haven't seen her with you before though. I'd keep her around all the time if I were you."

"Man, I wish I could, but she's heavy into her modeling career, and I only get to see her when she isn't working."

"Well, I'm sure you would if you could."

"Without a doubt. How about another drink, Jack."

"Sure. I think we can find something," I said as we headed toward the patio.

The party was going really well. I noticed that Gary and Cheryl were dancing and talking with people on the dance floor. Sandy and Kevin were by the pool talking with some of Willie's friends. As planned, we spent almost the entire evening with Willie and Michelle. Gabriella and Michelle seem to become instant friends. We would all dance awhile, drink awhile, then dance some more. At around three in the morning, with the party still going strong, Willie took me off the side.

"I'm sure you get high, man. How about you and I going inside for a quick one."

"Let's go up to my bedroom. No one will bother us, and I have my stash there," I directed, sensing that he was just drunk enough that he wasn't testing me. He really just wanted to get high. It was worth the risk and I took it.

"Lead the way, my man."

As we entered the bedroom, I told Willie to have a seat in a sofa chair by the window. I went over to the dresser and got a joint out of one of the drawers.

"You got a light, man?" I asked Willie as I handed him the marijuana.

"Yeah, man."

We sat there in the bedroom and smoked the whole thing. It was much more than I usually ever smoked. A couple of hits are all I can handle, but this was a special event. I was definitely tripping as we sat there.

"That's pretty good weed, man. You get that around here?"

"It's the last of the stuff I brought with me from Texas. I have one of my students picking me up some more, though."

"Jack, you should have come to me. I can get you anything you want."

"Hey, dude, I didn't know. Next time I will," I explained as we sat there and laughed.

"Give me just a minute, and we'll head back," he said as he reached in his back pocket and pulled out what looked like a cigarette case. He put it on the little table in front of us and opened it up. One side had a mirror and the other had a clear pouch that contains the white powder that I recognized immediately. He laid out four lines on the mirror, took a metal straw that was in the side of the case with the cocaine, and made two lines of H disappear without even batting an eye.

"This is excellent shit man. You need to try it," he said as he handed me the metal straw.

"Thanks anyway, Willie, but I can't control myself when I start using that stuff. I'll just stick to the weed. I hope you don't mind."

"That's cool, man, I understand. I can only handle it once in a while myself. I'm afraid I wouldn't make any money at all if I used it regular," he said laughing.

Bingo, I thought to myself, but restrained from saying anything at that point. "We better get back to the party. I know that there's one woman out there who will come looking for us soon."

"Yeah, and I know one that would help her."

As the party continued, it got closer and closer to daylight. Some of the guests were starting to go home. We were still going strong though. Gabriella took my hand and led me off to a quiet part of the patio. She put her arms around me and kissed me very passionately. I was ready to throw everyone out and make love to her right there.

"Jack, I have something to tell you and it's very important. Would you rather I wait till we're alone or tell you now?"

"Do I need to be sober to hear this or can I be like I am now?"

"If you're going to be mad at me, I'd rather have people around."

"Gabriella, there's nothing you could say that would ever make me mad."

"This might."

"Gabriella, tell me."

She looked up at me with tears in her eyes. I thought that I had done something wrong. "Jack, I love you, and I'm going to have your baby. Please don't be mad. I know we were going to wait, but it just happened."

I wasn't prepared for that at all. I thought about it for a couple of seconds as I stood there looking at this beautiful woman. The most important thing in the world to me was this woman, and she was worried about telling me about having our baby. I pulled away from her and took her hand.

"Gabriella, come with me," I said. I could feel the trembling in her hand. I lead her back over to where Willie and everyone else were. I let go of her hand and walked up to the microphone that the band had been using.

"Ladies and gentlemen, or those of us who are sober enough to listen, I have something important to tell you. This beautiful woman standing right here has just informed me that she has honored me more than any of you can possibly know. She is going to have our baby. Thank you, my darling," I said as I held out my hand to her smiling.

As she came to me, everyone began to applaud and go nuts. The liquor I guess. She was crying and smiling at the same time. I put my arms around her and held her very close.

"I knew you wouldn't be mad. I was just worried about the timing."

"Don't ever worry about anything, Gabriella. You're my wife and everything will always be OK. Let's see if we can get rid of all these people so that I can show you how much I love you."

"OK, but I don't think we'll be able to."

About that time, Willie, Michelle, and the rest of the guests bombarded us with congratulations. They lasted about another hour. Willie saved the best for the end.

"I guess we'll just have to have another party real soon to celebrate your potency, my man. As soon as I can arrange it, we're all going to fly down to Mexico City and have another celebration. That's OK with you, little mother to be?"

"Thank you, it sounds great."

"You can't have it until I can go," Michelle said.

"Then it's all set. A party to be determined soon. Congratulation my friends. A toast to the new baby."

"Thank you, Willie," Gabriella said with tears in her eyes.

"With that, I think we should all say our good-byes and leave this couple alone for a while," he said.

It was as if he had been a general in charge of troops. Everyone said goodnight and was gone within thirty minutes.

Gabriella and I locked up the house, and made our way to the bedroom. We took off our clothes, jumped in bed, and lay very close to each other without talking for a few minutes.

"Gabriella, you've made me very happy. I hope you know that."

"No way. You've made me very happy and I hope you know that."

We lay very quiet again, then turned toward each other and began laughing. We fell asleep in each other's arms.

I was sure it was daylight outside, because I could feel the rays from the sun through my closed eyelids. I was also sure that I was dreaming. I felt these very soft lips on my neck, kissing me very softly. They kept moving over my body. First to my chest and then my nipples. Then slowly down the center of my stomach, to my belly button. As these lips continued downward, I felt myself getting very hard, and I wished Gabriella was in my dream making this happen. As dreams go, I couldn't make out any face, but it was very exciting. I felt two hands gently caress my penis and massaging the whole area. This was getting better by the minute. I felt myself begin to move as the lips and the hands began to work together. As I felt the lips began to cover my very hard erection, I brought my hand down and began running it through the hair of the person in my dreams. She lowered her head over the entire thing in one quick gulp. I opened my eyes and Gabriella was doing it to me again. How could this woman do this to me?

"Gabriella, this ...isn't fair ...you...know."

She never even slowed down. She was very much into what she was doing. She also knew that when she was finished, she would get her reward. I had learned what really turned her on, and she would have several orgasms before I actually entered her for our big finish. Right now, I was doing a lousy job of controlling myself, and what had began as a dream was about to explode into ecstasy. In a matter of a few seconds, she was lying on top of me smiling.

"Good morning, darling. How did you like your wake up call?" she asked with that look she always has when she becomes mischievous.

"Woman, you have a talent that I wish I could some how put on the market. I'd be a millionaire. But now that you've took the strength out of me, I'll guess I just have to sleep for a little longer."

"I don't think so, mister," and she grabbed me and started massaging my penis again.

I smiled at her and rolled her over onto her back, "I don't think so either. It's my turn now."

"I knew that you were just kidding."

"You did, did you? Well, did you know that I was going to do this?" I said as I rolled her over onto her stomach and placed her arms above her head. "Now, don't move."

"Yes, sir."

I moved her hair over to one side and began to kiss the back of her neck. Working my way very slowly and systematically, I kissed each shoulder and ended up in the middle of her back. I gently kissed her again, and licked my way downward. There is this wonderful little place at the lowest part of her back, just before it reaches downward to her wonderful firm buttocks. Anyway, I stopped for a minute and laid my head there.

I could feel her breathing faster than normal, but a long way from where I was going to take her. As I lay there, I gently opened her legs very wide, and purposely let my hand come up the inside of her thighs. Now the breathing became faster. I ran my hand right into the place that in a matter of minutes, I would kiss and lick and she knew it was coming. I kind of circled the area with the tips of my finger and her breathing was getting heavier. It was already very moist there, and I knew she would have her first orgasm soon. I wanted to be there when she did. I moved my hand slowly up the middle of her buttocks to the small of her back, lifted my head, and began kissing her again. It was becoming more and more exciting for me too. I was kissing each cheek and lowering myself so that I could continue down each leg. After kissing both legs, I lowered myself off the bed almost in one motion, and without even stopping for air, I was on my knees in front of the bed. I was kissing the back of her heels and ankles and gently sliding her towards me. I was now kissing the inside of her thighs, and getting very close to where my hand had been only moments before. I gently kissed the moist spot and began using my tongue to excite her even more. I buried my head between her legs, and worked her through two orgasms before rolling her over and lying next to her for a brief minute of rest.

"Jack, now we're almost even."

"Gabriella, when we married, we created a new being out of the two of us, and since that happened, it's like this new being is growing by leaps and bounds. Even time doesn't count anymore. Every day that I spend with you, it's like the first day I fell in love with you. I love you, Gabriella, and I love our baby growing inside of you." I said holding her very close. The fragrance of her body was an odor that was heavenly, and I hated ever washing it off me.

Tears ran down her cheeks as she smile and said, "Jack, I have to steal a word from that movie *Ghost*—Ditto—I love you, too, and I can hardly wait till our baby is born."

We made love until we heard the doorbell ring. We just laughed at each other and I jumped out of bed, put on some shorts, and went to the door.

"Hi, Sandy. We forgot what time it was. Sorry to keep you waiting."

"It's OK, Jack. Gabriella needs all the rest she can get now."

"Yeah, she needs that too," I said winking at her.

"Don't tell me...you guys are disgusting," she said with a straight face. "Just kidding, I hope you two stay this happy forever."

"I'm sure we will. Come on in. Gabriella will be down in a few minutes. Can I get you something to drink?"

"I could use a cup of coffee, if its not too much trouble."

"No problem at all. It'll only take a few minutes to brew," I said as we walked to the kitchen. "Have a seat."

"Thanks, Jack. I'm still a little tired from last night. How you guys feeling?"

"I might have had just a little too much to drink."

"Might have!"

"OK, I had a lot to drink, but it was a great party. I also got a little closer to Willie."

"That's great. As soon as Cheryl and Gary get here we'll put our heads together for the next move."

"Hi, Sandy. Sorry to hold you guys up," Gabriella said walking into the kitchen.

"That's OK, Gabriella, we're still waiting for Cheryl and Gary anyway.

Gabriella came up to me, put her arms around me, and gave me a kiss. "How are you feeling my love."

"Fantastic."

"I'll finish making the coffee. Go sit down and keep Sandy company."

"You're the boss."

"Right," Gabriella said, and pinched me on the behind.

I sat down and continued talking with Sandy while Gabriella finished the coffee and brought it to the table. "Thanks, honey. What do you take in your coffee, Sandy?"

"Cream and sugar, if its not too much trouble."

"I'll get it, Gabriella. You sit and rest," I said as I went to the refrigerator, got some milk, and sat back down.

"I'm not tired, Jack...Well, not because of the baby," she said, and we laughed.

"What about that guy I saw you hanging out with last night, Sandy. I mean, he wasn't the guy you came with, was he?"

"Kevin was busy with some girl, and I got to talking with this guy who works for Willie. His name is Bill something and I think he's pretty close to Willie. At least I saw him with Willie most of the night. Anyway, I have a date with him next weekend," she explained.

"He's got a great ass," Gabriella said laughing.

"Yeah, I know," and Sandy joined in laughing.

"Gabriella, you never said I have a great ass."

"It'll do for what I need."

"And what's that, my dear?"

"I'll show you later," she said and they were laughing again.

"Enough said."

Just about then the doorbell rang. I got up and went to the door. "It's about time you guys got here. What have you been up to?" They looked at each other. I was sure they were up to the same thing Gabriella and I had been doing.

"Just trying to recoup from last night," Cheryl said.

"That was a hell of a party, Jack," Gary added.

"Are you sure that's all you guys have been doing since last night?" I asked and I caught a look from Gary that didn't need explaining. "Never mind. We're in the kitchen having coffee. You guys want a cup?"

"I'll have one," Cheryl said.

"That sounds great," Gary stated.

"Hey, guys. You two seemed to have survived the party," Sandy said.

"Too much free booze for me," Gary said.

"Congratulations again, Gabriella. I know you can't wait for the baby to be here," Cheryl said as she gave Gabriella a big hug.

"Thank you, Cheryl. You're right, I can hardly wait. Jack and I had talked about it, but we weren't planning on having one right now. The pill doesn't always work."

"It'll be just fine, Gabriella. This will all be over long before the baby is born," Cheryl added.

"We sure hope so."

"Speaking of getting this over with, we better get busy so we can make sure this is wrapped up soon, long before your baby is born," Sandy said.

"It has to be, Sandy. Let's go out by the pool. The sun will do us all some good," I added knowing that there might be a chance the house was bugged.

We made our way to the pool and Sandy began a discussion about the previous night.

"What I'd like to start with is to let everyone give their analysis of the party. What they found out, and what we can do."

"Have another party," Cheryl said laughing.

"Yeah," I said as we all started laughing.

"Seriously guys. What can we do next? Let's start with you, Cheryl," Sandy said.

"Well, Gary and I spent most of the night talking with staff at the university. It seems that the president, Matt, and his wife may be involved with Willie's operation. It might be best if we concentrate on them."

"Yeah, they were all getting high and were kidding around most of the night. We didn't find out anything definite, but I'm sure they're involved somehow," Gary added.

"I noticed that they were awful chummy, too," Gabriella stated.

"OK, then I suggest you and Gary work on Matt and his wife. What's her name, anyway?" Sandy asked.

"I think it's Sue," Gabriella said.

"Yeah, that's it," Gary stated.

"See if they are just using, or if they have money invested in it," Sandy directed.

"That shouldn't be hard to find out," Cheryl said.

"Jack, we already know you and Gabriella are working on Willie, but did you find out anything that we should know?" Sandy asked.

"There are a couple of things that might be important. When we went to our bedroom, of course we both got high, but he pulled out some coke and did it in front of me without any hesitation. I hinted around that I might be interested in some pot, and I'm sure that won't be any problem. Gabriella and I should start working on doing some minor buying, and working our way up," I stated.

"Maybe you should buy a bag next week, and a couple of days later approach him about a bigger buy," Sandy questioned.

"I think within a couple of weeks, I can be working on some big money deals. Should I work right into the coke thing?"

"Absolutely. That's really what we need to put him away. Don't waste much time on pot."

"Will there be any problem getting the money we need?" I asked. I knew it was a dumb question, but I wanted to know how long it would take to get it together.

"We can get any amount of money you need within twelve hours," Sandy said.

"Then that's what Gabriella and I will work on."

"What else have you got," Sandy asked.

"Well, that girl, Michelle, that Willie brought. There's something familiar about her. I don't know what it is, but I feel as though I know her from somewhere. I got that same thing from her. I'm sure she thinks she knew me from somewhere."

"I guess we better check her out. I'll let you know. If you figure it out let me know. We don't want her to screw things up now."

"I'm sure she wasn't involved in the Florida deal, but there's something."

"It better not be an old girlfriend," Gabriella said.

Everyone turned to her and started laughing. "Do you really think you need to worry," Gary said.

"You never know," Gabriella said and looked at me.

Gary, Sandy, and I looked at each other, and in almost the same breath said, "nah..." and burst out laughing.

"Well, I'd kick her ass if she ever got any ideas," Gabriella said with that girlish look.

"Honey, don't worry."

"I'm not worried. I'll never let you go anyway."

I gave her a quick kiss and said, "I love you."

Then Sandy started, "I'm going to work on Bill. That tall guy I was telling you about."

"What are you going to work on?" I said and poked at her.

"You know what I mean."

"I was just kidding."

"OK. That should just about do it. The only other things I want to mention are that we know Willie has already checked you out Jack, and I don't think we should meet at any of our houses any more," Sandy said.

"Don't forget about the phones. The ones at home and at your office," Cheryl added.

"Good idea, Cheryl. We should be even more careful now. The next month or so will make or break us." Sandy said.

"Maybe we shouldn't meet as a group anymore," Gary added.

"Absolutely! Only a couple of us together at any given time. Does anyone have anything else," Sandy asked.

"I have something," Gabriella said.

"What's that, Gabriella?"

"I think we should get something to eat. I'm hungry."

We all started laughing and that ended our meeting by deciding we'd go out for something to eat.

27

*B*Y THE FOLLOWING FRIDAY, I HAD ALREADY bought my first bag of pot from Willie, and had discussed the possibility of more. I was in my office grading papers and someone knocked on my door. "Come in."

"Hi, Jack, how are you doing," Michelle said.

"Hi, Michelle. I never expected to see you here."

"You never know who'll turn up, do you?"

"I guess not. What are you doing back in town?"

"I got some time off from work. Willie and I are flying to Mexico for the weekend."

"That sounds like fun. What part?"

"Mexico City. That's where his relatives are."

"Oh yeah. I remember him saying that now."

I was really starting to wonder what she was doing in my office.

"We're leaving in the morning. He doesn't know I'm here yet. I'm going to surprise him."

She still said nothing about why she was in my office, and again I got that feeling that I knew her from somewhere.

"Are you looking for a place to hide for awhile?"

"No. Nothing like that."

"Did I do something when I was drunk the other night?"

"No. It has nothing to do with that. We do need to discuss something though."

"OK. I give up. What can I do for you?"

"I want you to look at this picture and tell me what you think."

"OK" and she hands me the picture.

As I looked at this picture she handed me, I couldn't believe what I was seeing. It was a picture of this young couple and a small baby. I knew who it was instantly. "These friends of yours, Michelle?"

"The woman in the picture is my mother."

I did all I could to control my reaction, but I knew that she could tell I was in complete shock. After a few seconds, the only thing I could think to say was, "She's very beautiful. How old were you in the picture?"

"I was only eight months at the time."

She had everything down right so far.

"You were a beautiful baby, too. What's this got to do with me?"

"I think you're the man in the picture...."

"Come on, Michelle. What gives you that idea?"

"I looked at that picture all my life, and wondered who he might be. When I saw you the other night, I called my mom and told her I thought it might be you."

"What did she say?"

"Told me I was crazy. That my dad was some place in Florida."

"Well then, that answers that."

"No. There is one way we can be sure."

"How?"

"My real father has a tattoo on his right arm with two hearts. See it here in the picture," and she pointed to it on this guy's arm. "Can I please see your right arm?"

This was something I hadn't expected. What do I do now? There wasn't enough time to think of a good excuse. "Lots of people have tattoos like that."

"Jack, the names are covered up. My mom said that they were my dad's name and his old girlfriend. I have to know for sure, Jack."

There was nothing I could do but roll up my sleeve.

"You are my father, aren't you?" she said looking at my arm.

"Yes, Michelle. I'm your father." I couldn't believe what had just taken place. I hadn't seen her or her mother since that picture was taken. We had decided not to marry because we weren't in love. I had moved to Florida and never heard another word. How could she turn up now and at this time? The whole program might have to end if I didn't think of something quick.

"It was your eyes that gave you away. They still had that same glow in them that I saw in the picture. It was just fate that we ran into each other."

"You sure said a mouthful. I never expected to see you at all. You really have turned out to be a very beautiful woman."

"Thank you. You know it's funny. I was planning on going to Florida this summer to look for you. Mom said you had a brother that lived down there. I do have a question for you though. Why are you going by the last name of Cannon?"

"Michelle, it's a very long story, and I'm not sure you have time right now," I said for lack of a better response. What to do now. "I do want to explain as soon as you have time."

"I really want to know."

"I had this strange feeling when we first met that I knew you, but I never dreamed."

"I thought I'd never get to meet you. Mom said you were a wonderful man, but I wanted to know for myself."

"There's a lot about me that you need to know, and I have a special favor to ask you. It's a two-part favor and I have to ask it."

"I'll try to give you a two-part answer," she said smiling.

"Well, are you in love with Willie?"

"Does it matter?"

"Yes, maybe."

"I'm not sure. We haven't known each other very long, but we are very close. Why?"

"That leads to my second question, and I'm asking you this because I need time to explain all this to Gabriella. Would you not say anything about us until I've talked to Gabriella, but most important until I have time to talk with you?"

She stood there for a few minutes and just stared out the window. Finally she turned towards me and said, "I didn't come here to create problems for you. I just wanted to meet my real father. For that reason, we'll make it our secret. I won't even tell Mom. Now, I have a favor to ask."

"Anything."

"I want to give you a hug, and you tell me everything can be normal between us, now that I found you," she said as tears formed in her eyes and she began to cry.

I walked over to her, put my arms around her and whispered, "Everything will be fine, Michelle, I promise."

"Thank you, Daddy," she said as she pulled away. "It is OK for me to call you that, isn't it?"

"You better."

I talked with Michelle for about another fifteen minutes or so before she had to meet with Willie. I found out that she had stayed in Alabama until she left for UCLA. That was where she got into modeling. Her mom was married and happy, and she had two brothers. Her modeling career was very successful and getting better. There were still a million questions that we had to ask each other, but they would have to wait.

"Call me when you back home, and I'll try to set up a time so we can be together. Remember not to discuss this ...."

She looked at me with those big brown eyes and interrupted saying, "Daddy, I promised. Don't worry."

We hugged each other again and she left the office.

28

I SAT IN MY OFFICE FOR THE NEXT HOUR trying to decide just how I was going to handle this situation. I knew that I must tell Gabriella immediately, but from that point I had no idea what to do. I was almost positive that Sandy would pull the plug on the whole operation. And what was I going to do about this daughter of mine. She deserved to be acknowledged, and she deserved my love. I left the office with only the hope that Gabriella could help me decide how to handle this.

"How was your day, my love?"

"I can tell you one thing. I always thought you to be one of the most beautiful women in the world, but I was wrong. That life you carry inside of you has made you even more beautiful. I never knew that it could be possible, but you are the most beautiful part of the world, and I'm glad to be in it."

"Jack." She began to cry. "Everyone is going to see me crying. Couldn't you have waited until we got home to tell me that." She laid her head on my shoulder and we rode the rest of the way home in silence.

When we got home, the phone was ringing, and Gabriella ran ahead to answer it.

"Hello."

"Gabriella, I'm glad I caught you guys at home. How are you feeling?" the voice on the other end asked.

"Hello, Willie. I'm feeling wonderful."

"Great, you and Jack pack a bag. We're going to Mexico for the weekend."

"That sounds like fun. Let me get you Jack," she said, and handed me the phone.

"Jack, pack a bag, We're going to Mexico."

"Willie, I think we can arrange it, but could you give us about thirty minutes so we can run to the store?"

"Jack, just pack a bag. We'll be there in fifteen minutes. We can stop at the store on the way."

"OK, Willie, we'll be ready," I said, and hung up the phone.

"Jack, I guess we're going off for the weekend."

"If you don't want to go, I'll call him back."

"No ... I want to go. It'll be fun, and isn't that what we're here for?"

"Well, I guess we'd better pack."

"I guess we better. By the way, I love you, Jack."

"Gabriella, someone ought to write a book about how much I love you."

"I don't think anyone could put it in words."

"You're probably right. We better hurry. Willie will be here in a minute, and we need to get in touch with Sandy."

"I'll call her while you get the suitcases. OK?"

"Be careful what you say on the phone. They may already have our lines tapped. We have to be careful."

"I will. Just get us the two small suitcases."

"OK."

It was about 6:00 P.M. when the private jet took off from the airport. Gabriella had contacted Sandy and let her know what was going on, but there was little time for anything else. We were basically on our own if anything went wrong. What if Michelle had told Willie about me? What if she was more involved than she had said? What about Gabriella? If anything happens to her because I hesitated to tell her and Sandy. I looked out the window of the jet and prayed a silent prayer.

"What's wrong, Jack?"

"Nothing honey. I'm just a little tired. I think I'll take a short nap. Wake me up in about an hour." That's all I could think to do until we were somewhere alone, so I could explain to Gabriella. I didn't want her to worry. I closed my eyes and tried to make some sort of plans. I heard Willie, Michelle, and Gabriella discussing what we were going to do in Mexico City. Everything sounded very normal to this point.

Our jet landed three hours later and Willie had a limo waiting for us at the airport. We went to the Hilton Hotel in the downtown area, and of course Willie got us rooms on the top floor. I couldn't believe that he actually took twelve rooms. One for us, one for him and Michelle, and the rest were for friends and bodyguards, or whatever they were.

"Well Jack, are you ready to do some more partying," Willie said as we were almost to our rooms.

"You bet. What time are we going out?"

"I thought we'd give the ladies time to get ready. How about an hour?"

"That's plenty for me," Gabriella said.

"Yeah, me too," Michelle added.

"OK then, one hour, and we'll meet in the lounge downstairs," Willie stated.

"See you in an hour," I said as we enter our room.

I thought I was walking into a house. It had five large rooms. A bedroom with a king-size bed, a bathroom with a separate shower, a hot tub, and bath, a setting room, and another bedroom. Oh yes, and a fully equipped kitchen.

"Isn't this beautiful, Jack.?"

"We could really get spoiled."

Gabriella walked over to the balcony, and just stood there looking out at the ocean. I walked up and put my arms around her from behind. She folded her arms over mine and said in a very soft voice, "Does this remind you of anything?"

"How could I forget that night. Sometimes I wish we were back in Florida. It was a lot simpler then."

"But I'm not sure that we'd be together if we were still in Florida."

"Maybe not, but I would still be in love with you."

"I know you would. I'm just not sure I would have been. It took you leaving for me to realize that I loved you, too."

"You know I always told you that we were meant to be together, and I don't think even you could have kept us apart for long."

"I know Jack," she said. We just stood there for a what seemed like forever. Then she turned around and held me very close, burying her head in my chest. "I remembered having all these stupid excuses why it wouldn't work for us."

"What happened?" I said, already knowing what she was going to say.

"I realized that all my excuses were just that. When you were away from me, I knew that I couldn't live without you."

"There wasn't anything I could have done to make you change your mind, was there?"

"At that point, probably not."

"I didn't think so."

"We better get ready or we'll be late."

"Just one more thing."

"Yes, I love you and no, I don't have any regrets."

The weekend went by so fast that I didn't have time to tell Gabriella what had taken place in my office. We had a wonderful time, and Michelle kept her word. If she didn't, Willie wasn't letting on at all. So I decided just to wait and explain when we returned home. I had managed to talk with Willie about investing some money in his operations, however.

"Jack, how much money do you have that I can put to work for you?"

"Willie, it really depends on the return, and how quick it all happens."

"The turnover is almost immediate and with almost no risk at all."

"Can you handle around a hundred thousand?"

"You're pretty serious about this, I take it."

"I want to retire and play."

"Not to worry, my friend, we're going to play."

"I'll have the money for you Monday."

"We'll make it work."

"Oh yeah, can you get me a pound of grass?"

"Sure. I'll have it when you drop off the money."

"How much?"

"Three hundred and fifty dollars."

"Deal."

The ball was rolling. All I had to do was get with Sandy and the operation was taking shape. The only other thing that happened that weekend was a few minutes that Michelle and I talked. I even noticed that Willie and Gabriella might have gotten a little jealous.

"Michelle, I think Gabriella and Willie are watching us a little too close," I said to her while we were dancing at one of the many clubs we went to that weekend.

"You haven't talked to Gabriella yet, I take it."

"I haven't had a chance."

"She's very beautiful. Where did you meet her?"

"Teaching in Florida."

"I should have known."

"You're beautiful, too."

"Thank you, Daddy."

"Are we going to be able to talk soon?"

"I have a major shoot coming up, but after that we'll get together. I'll give you a call."

"Thanks for giving me time to tell Gabriella."

"I'm just glad I finally got to meet you."

"They're watching us again."

"If they only knew."

"How do you think Gabriella will accept me?"

"She's the most understanding person I've ever met, and I know she'll love you."

"I sure hope so."

That was the extent of our conversation that weekend. The rest of the weekend we just partied. As soon as we got back Sunday night and Willie dropped us off at home, Gabriella and I rode to the convenience store and phoned Sandy.

"Sandy, I need to talk to you tonight."

"I'll meet you at the Village Inn in thirty minutes."

"OK."

We drove to the restaurant, went in, and sat down. I began to tell Gabriella about the deal Willie and I had going. Just as I finished telling Gabriella, Sandy came walking in. I had to go through the whole thing again with Sandy.

"I'll have the money for you first thing in the morning. Are you sure this isn't a set up?"

"It was all his idea. I just suggested the amount. I mean it could be, but we still have to take the chance. How will I get the money from you?"

"It'll be in your account in the morning. All I have to do is make the call."

"I'll drop you off at work in the morning, and bring you the money at lunch," Gabriella added.

"Did he ask for any certain denominations?" Sandy questioned.

"Not at all. I just need an extra $350 for a pound of pot. Is that a problem?"

"It'll be there. Just be careful. What time is the exchange?"

"He said tomorrow night."

"That's great Jack. Everything is moving along well. It won't be long now and you two can get into a normal relationship."

"Sandy, being with Jack is anything but normal, and I love it that way."

"Well, we all need to get some sleep. Remember, be very careful," Sandy warned.

"We're going to be just fine," I said and my mind wander back to Michelle. I hope we could get this all done and not have her involved.

The next day everything went well getting the money. That evening Gabriella and I were sitting at home waiting for Willie to call when the doorbell rang. When I opened the door there was Willie and that guy Bill that Sandy had been talking with at the party.

"I figured you guys might be a little tired from the weekend, so I thought I'd just stop by. I hope I didn't catch you at a bad time."

"Come on in. I was just sitting here waiting for you to call, Willie."

"Well then, I just saved you the trip. Are we all set for our little business deal."

"Yeah, I have the money right here," and I pointed at the briefcase.

"Great. This will be a quick turnaround so be ready to put some of that back in circulation in about a week."

"Now that sounds great."

"Bill, go to the car and bring the stuff in the console."

"OK, Willie," Bill said, and he went to the car and returned in a matter of seconds.

"Hi, Willie," Gabriella said as she entered the room.

"Gabriella. You look radiant as usual," Willie said as he kissed her on the cheek.

"Thank you. Are you guys about through with your business?"

"Just about, honey," I said.

"Do you have time for a cup of coffee or something?"

"Thanks for the offer, Gabriella, but I have some business to take care of tonight. Can I take a rain check?"

"Willie, you don't even have to ask."

"I figured that's what you'd say. Jack, don't worry about a thing. Your money is safer with me than being in the bank. No offense, Gabriella."

"We aren't worried," Gabriella said and then added, "We just want to make some money to retire."

"Then we'll have no problems. Jack, here's your stuff. Let me know what you think," Willie said as he handed me the pot.

"Bill, I noticed you and Sandy from the university really hit it off," Gabriella said.

"Yeah, she's a lot of fun."

"I talked to her today and you were all she talked about. Have you called her?"

"Not yet, but I plan to. She talked about me, huh?"

"I wouldn't wait too long to call her. There are a lot of guys asking her out." Gabriella said as I was inspecting the pot.

"I'll call her. We've been a little busy."

"Ever since Gabriella and I have been together, she has been trying to play cupid. I think she hopes everyone can have the kind of relationship we have," I continued.

"It's possible, Jack. Isn't that what you've always told me?" she said as she held my arm.

"She's right. Anything is possible."

"Well Jack, I wish we could stay longer, but we have business. Maybe we can get together later in the week and have dinner," Willie said, extending his hand. It was the kind of a shake that seals a deal.

"We wish you could hang around, but we understand."

"You just take care of this beautiful woman," Willie added as he kissed Gabriella on the cheek and they made their exit.

After they pulled away, I turned to Gabriella and said, "You're really getting into this thing, aren't you?"

"What do you mean?" she asked as she turned to face me at the front door. I could tell by the look in her eyes that she knew exactly what I was talking about. She always knew what I was thinking. It still amazed me at how suitable we were for one another.

"You know exactly what I mean."

"Listen here, buster. We women are good at that kind of stuff. Besides, we got to speed this up some, now that I'm pregnant."

"See what I mean."

"You're right, and you know how hard it is for me to admit that," she said laughing.

"I know it had to hurt."

"What time will Gary be here?"

"I'll have to call him."

The plan was for Gary and me to bag the pot up, and Gary would sell it around the campus. That would make us that much more believable. We had to make sure they knew we were involved and we were sure Willie would have someone watching. He didn't get where he was by being stupid.

"How long will it take for you guys to bag it?"

"Only about an hour."

"Good, I'm getting very tired."

"Why don't you go lay down, and I'll wake you when I come to bed."

"Are you sure you won't mind?" she said with that little-girl look of hers.

"Gabriella."

"OK, promise you'll wake me up when you come to bed."

"Yes, I promise." I knew I had to talk to her about Michelle before it got any further, and it might take a while. A nap was just what she needed. As she turned to walk away from me, I called out her name, "Gabriella."

She turned back around with her hands on her hip, "How am I going to get any rest if you don't let me get to the bedroom." She had a stern look on her face, but I knew she was kidding.

"I just want to...."

She interrupted me right there. "I love you too, darling." She walked back over to me and gave me a kiss. "Now let me get some rest. I'll have something special for you later."

I knew she would too. I wish I had written a book about our love. It would have to be good, if I could only put it into words. "Back to business," I thought to myself. I picked up the phone and called Gary.

"Hello," a woman said on the other end of the line. The voice sounded very familiar.

"Can I speak to Gary?"

Who ever answered the phone put that hand over the receiver because the next voice I heard was Gary's, "Hey, Jack, you ready man?"

"Yeah."

"See ya."

Cheryl had come with Gary, and we all sat in the kitchen bagging up the pot. When we were just about finished, Gary said, "I'll have this all distributed in a couple of days and your money back within the week."

"That's great, man. As soon as you get that done, I'll get another one. How much do you think we'll make?"

"Close to a thousand."

"Maybe I can quit teaching before long."

"Only after we've made as much as we did in Texas."

"Right."

He was carrying this whole thing out to a T. If they were listening to us in the house, they were hearing just what they needed to hear.

"How's Gabriella feeling, Jack?" Cheryl asked.

"She got a little tired tonight, but I think she's still too excited to get real tired yet. It won't be long though."

"How about you?" she asked.

"I'm tired, too," I laughed.

"You know what I mean. Are you excited?"

"I can hardly wait. This baby will be so spoiled. No one will be able to be around her."

"Her?"

"Well, I mean. Whatever it is," I said laughing.

"What do you prefer? Boy or girl?" Gary asked.

"Healthy mother and baby."

"Just so the baby looks like Gabriella and not you," Gary said.

"You got that right," Cheryl added.

"You know we're right. That's what makes it so bad," Gary said with a smile.

We just laughed.

As Gary was packing everything into his sports bag, I just had to ask Cheryl, "You and Gary sure are spending a lot of time together. I know it's not any of my business, but he's my friend."

"What am I, your enemy?" she said smiling.

"You're my friend, too. You know what I mean. But what about you and Gary?"

"I think you ought to ask him."

"Well, Gary?"

"She can't keep her hands off me. I've tried everything."

"Let's see who keeps whose hands off who," Cheryl added with that very serious look of hers. She can look so mean sometimes, but she has a heart of gold.

"I was just kidding, honey."

"Boy, this is getting serious, isn't it?" I observed.

"It just kind of happened, if you know what I mean," Gary stated.

"Are you kidding?"

"He's lucky I even let him hang around," Cheryl added with a very serious look on her face.

"I said I was just kidding," Gary said, trying to look very pitiful.

"So was I," Cheryl stated.

"Hey, I'm sorry I started this argument. I won't ask again."

"We're just kidding, Jack. Gary and I enjoy spending time together, so we do."

"Lots of time together. I think it's time for us to be together again now, don't you?" Gary added, leaning over and giving her a kiss.

"I think you're right. Jack, tell Gabriella we're sorry we didn't get to see her, will you?"

"Sure."

"Tell her I'll give her a call tomorrow."

"OK."

"We'd stay longer Jack, but you look real tired," Gary said, picking up his bag and heading toward the door.

"Yeah right. I'm getting real tired," I said winking at Cheryl. She just smiled.

"Well, I guess you better let me get some rest. I'll call you tomorrow Gary."

"Sure man, no problem," Gary said as they were walking out the door.

I locked the door and turned off the lights. I tiptoed into the bedroom. The TV set was on, and Gabriella was sound asleep. I took off my clothes and slid under the covers beside her. I didn't want to disturb her. She look so peaceful, and just moaned as I slide my arm up under her and pulled her very close to me. I laid there very quietly just holding her. On the TV there was a movie just ending. George Strait was singing this song called "I Cross My Heart." I had to wake Gabriella so she could hear this. I gently kissed her on the lips. She jumped just a little until she realized it was me.

"I love you, Jack."

"I love you, Gabriella. Listen to this song. It's beautiful."

She sat up in the bed so she could watch the TV. George Strait was on stage in Las Vegas and walked to the end of the runway and sang this song. The lady he sang it to had tears in her eyes. When he finished, he walked down the stairs, and the movie ended with them holding each other. Gabriella was crying quietly and buried her head in my chest.

"We have to get the CD with that song on it, Jack."

"Tomorrow."

We then made love for what could have been thirty minutes or three hours. Time wasn't the important thing. Being one again was. It was that other being coming to life again I talked about before. That two that become one. I love this woman and she loved me.

We lay very quiet when we finished, just holding each other. I knew that I had to tell her about Michelle soon or she would be sound asleep again. She began to breathe deeply and slowly, and I knew that she was just about asleep.

"There's something I need to talk to you about before you fall asleep."

"Couldn't it wait 'til morning? I'm very tired."

"Gabriella, I'd better tell you now."

With that she sat up in the bed and looked me in the eyes. "What's wrong, Jack?"

"It's not that bad, honey. Let's go sit out by the pool, and I'll tell you all about it."

"OK."

We threw on some clothes and made our way to the pool, and sat down in the lounge chairs. She had a very worried look on her face, and I wanted to calm her down as quickly as possible.

I lit a cigarette, which she hated me to do, and said to her, "Please let me tell you the whole story before you ask questions, OK?"

"Jack, quit bullshitting and tell me."

I began to tell her the whole story about Michelle up to the time we got back from the trip to Mexico. When I finish I said, "Now, you can ask questions."

She sat there for few minutes still digesting all this. Then she said, "Are you sure she's your daughter?"

"Yes."

"Are you sure she hasn't said anything to Willie?"

"Pretty sure. At least for now."

"Have you told Sandy yet?"

"I wanted to tell you first to see how you think we ought to handle it."

"Thank you, honey. I know that when you tell Sandy, she'll cancel the whole operation."

"I know. I don't want to quit here. We've gotten pretty close now."

"Maybe we should just wait and see how Michelle will handle it when you explain the whole thing to her."

"Sandy could get us out of here before she had a chance to tell Willie."

"We'd be taking a big risk," Gabriella added.

"I just worry about you."

"I feel safe as long as you're here with me."

"So you think we should wait?"

"Yes," she said and she looked like she wanted to add something.

"And?"

"And, I love you. Let's wait a while longer and see what happens before we tell Sandy."

"I don't deserve someone like you."

"Oh yes, you do." She said laughing. "Now let's go to bed. I mean let's go to sleep."

"Are you sure"

"Only about the bed part," she said.

29

*T*HE WEEKS WENT BY VERY QUICKLY. Just as Willie had promised, my invest-
ment was back by the first weekend, and I had told him to just let it ride.
I also had him get another pound of marijuana, since Gary had distributed
all of the other one. Gary and Cheryl were becoming more and more
involved. It was great seeing them together. Gabriella was starting to show
signs of being pregnant. Her breasts were getting larger and her stomach
wasn't as flat as it had been. She looked more radiant with each passing
day. I hadn't heard anything from Michelle, but she had said that she
would be busy for awhile.

"Jack, it's time that we try and push things forward. Can you get Willie
to sell to you direct?" Sandy asked.

"I agree with you. I think he's about ready to do anything with me."

"I think he will, Sandy."

"We've seen or talked with him almost every day, and he said we could
do more when we're ready," Gabriella added.

"Have you and Bill been dating?" Cheryl asked Sandy

"Yeah. He really is a perfect gentleman, and I hate to bust him, but...."

"When we start busting people, we're going to get a lot of prominent
people," Gary stated.

"How many do you estimate are involved in Willie's operation?"
Gabriella asked.

"More than a hundred, including your boss at the university," Sandy
said looking at me.

"It was obvious with him. He lets everyone know what he's doing,"
Gary said.

"Matt uses more than he could ever make."

"He'll get plenty of help where he's going. I estimate that he's selling
about half a million a month," Sandy continued.

"It's got to be at least that much," Cheryl said.

"We've got the mayor and a couple of the commissioners, plus about a third of the police force," Sandy said.

"Well, we'd better get the ball rolling. I'm going to tell him I want to buy a million in coke, and tell him that I'll have to be there for the exchange, right?"

"That's the plan," Sandy said.

"When do we set it up?" Gabriella asked.

"After the next turn around. That should be this weekend, right?" Sandy asked.

"Yeah, unless something changes."

"OK, set it up. I'll make all the arrangements on my end," Sandy stated.

"Where do we meet to get the money?"

"Jack, I think we ought to meet at another restaurant. The waitresses are starting to call us by our first names," Gary said laughing.

"I agree. Let's make it that bar just off campus. What's the name of it?" Sandy asked.

"Buffalo Bills," Cheryl stated.

"OK. Then, that's it," Sandy said.

30

*S*ATURDAY AFTERNOON WILLIE CALLED and invited us to his house for a cook-out that night. I still hadn't heard anything from Michelle, and he didn't say whether she would be there or not. When we got to Willie's house there were cars everywhere. It looked like half the town was at his home. As I pulled into the driveway and stopped, one of my students came up.

"I'll park that for you, Mr. Cannon," the guy said with a big smile.

"Thanks, Robert. It looks like quite a big party."

"Yeah, Willie knows how to throw a party. Hi, Mrs. Cannon. You look great."

"Thank you, Robert. Are you gonna get to party any?"

"Willie doesn't allow that kind of stuff, but he pays damn good, so who cares."

"Right. Where do we go, Robert?"

"Just ring the bell, Mr. Cannon. Willie has been waiting for you."

"Thanks."

We walked up to the door and I rang the bell. This guy, about seven feet tall, opens the door and says, "Well, Mr. Cannon, come on in."

"Thanks."

"I just need to take a minute of your time." He begins to run this metal detector down my pants leg.

"Pedro, I told you to bring the Cannons to me as soon as they arrived. Forget the detector. Got it?" Willie said.

"Right, Willie, I just...."

"Never mind. Jack, it's about time. Gabriella, you're getting more and more beautiful."

"Thanks, Willie."

"Hey, man, you said eight o'clock," I added in defense.

"I said about eight."

"Well."

"Hey, man, just kidding. It's time to party," he said, and we both laughed.

"Then we better get started."

"Just follow me, my friends."

His house was three times the size of ours, and that was just the bottom floor. When we finally made it to the back of the house, there must have been one hundred-fifty people standing around either talking or dancing. There were a few people in the hot tub, and a few swimming in his Olympic-size pool. There was still plenty of room in his compound for two or three hundred more. It was huge. There were women wearing next to nothing, walking around serving drinks. You noticed right away who the guys were that were working for Willie as security. They all dressed casually, but had radios, and weren't drinking anything.

As Willie walked us around the area, he stopped and introduced us to everyone. Over at the hot tub, we ran into Bill and Sandy, who were with Gary and Cheryl. They ask us to join them, and we promised to return soon. All the people that we had talked about at the restaurant were there. All we have had to do was back up the busses and load them up. Case closed.

We joined right in with everything that was going on. Willie and I had already smoked a joint. Gabriella and I danced and mingled. Then we danced some more.

"Jack, have you seen Michelle anywhere?" Gabriella asked.

"Nowhere."

"That's good."

"You're right about that."

Just as soon as Gabriella finished that, I turned around and up walked Michelle.

"Hello, Jack. Sorry I'm so late getting here, but we just finished shooting. Willie had his jet waiting for me and here I am. Hi, Gabriella. How's the baby coming?"

"Hi, Michelle. The baby and I are just great."

"You look great."

"You do too, thanks."

Michelle leaned up to my ear and whispered, "Have you told her yet?"

"Yes, and everything is fine."

"That's great. I'll call you Monday."

"OK."

"I've got to find Willie. I'll see you two later."

"Come back and talk with me, Michelle," Gabriella said.

"Oh, we have a lot to talk about," she said laughing, and she turned to begin her search for Willie.

"Gabriella, she looks like she is stoned out of her mind. You be careful what you stay to her, OK."

"I'll be careful, Jack. Don't worry."

Everything was going fine. There was plenty of food and lots to drink. Everyone was dancing or swimming. Willie and I had smoked another joint, and I noticed that Gabriella and Michelle were sitting on lawn chairs talking.

"I guess you were a little surprised when Jack told you about me," Michelle said.

"That's an understatement. I imagine that Jack was a little surprised, too, wasn't he?" Gabriella asked.

"If you consider how big the United States are and the likelihood of us running into one another...."

Gabriella interpreted, "It must be fate."

"That's the way it was when I met Willie."

"What happened?"

"I fell in love with him the minute I saw him."

"How long have you two been dating?"

"Almost a year. How long have you and Jack been married?"

"Almost a year."

"You guys didn't waste any time deciding to have a baby."

"We really didn't plan on having one right now, but it turned out all right."

"It sure did."

"Michelle, we better get back over to the guys. I noticed that Willie was looking over here quite a bit."

"He can't stand to be away from me."

They turned and walked back over to us, and I caught a strange look on Gabriella's face. Something had to be wrong. I leaned down and kissed her cheek, and then whispered in her ear, "Is everything all right?"

"I'm not feeling very well, Jack. Can we go home soon?"

"Sure, honey. Give a few minutes me with Willie, and then I'll be ready to go."

"Yeah, but please hurry."

I turned and walked over to where Willie was standing and said, "Willie, can I talk to you a minute? Gabriella isn't feeling well, and I think we have to leave pretty soon."

"Sure, Jack, let's go over by the pool. There's only a couple of people there now. Is Gabriella all right?'

"I'm sure she's just tired because of the baby."

We stopped at the far end of the pool and Willie said, "Is there a problem, man?"

"Not hardly. I just wanted to ask you about investing some more money. It's not making me much in the bank, and I kind of like this upper-echelon life."

"How much we talking, my man."

"One mil."

"Where did you get all that money? Not on a teacher's salary, I'm sure."

"I did a little dealing back in Texas."

"Well, I'm sure I can handle that. Just give me a call. Now, get back over there and take your beautiful wife home."

"Thanks, man, I'll call you tomorrow."

I walked back over to Gabriella and she stood up. We started making our way to the door. It took about ten minutes, because we had to say good-bye to everyone.

When we finally got in the car, Gabriella told me what was bothering her.

"She told me that they were more than just friends."

"The day she came by the office, she sounded like she couldn't make up her mind whether she was in love with him or not."

"Well, tonight she told me that she had been in love with him since she first met him."

"I just wish I knew if she was going to tell him or not. Maybe when I talk to her Monday, I'll know more."

"I think it's time we told Sandy what is going on, don't you, Jack?"

"Gabriella, we're so close. Maybe I can put off telling Sandy anything for a week or so, and by then we'll have everything set up."

"All she has to do is mention to Willie that you guys are related, and the whole thing is over anyway. Jack, I think it's time to tell Sandy."

She has that manner about her that lets me know this wasn't one of those discussion statements. I had been with this woman long enough to know what she was thinking before she said it. I'm good at it, but she is uncanny.

"Jack, tell her tomorrow." I was right. End of discussion.

"OK, honey, I'll see her tomorrow. I don't want anything happening to you and our baby."

She leaned over and kissed me on the cheek as we pulled into the drive way. She put her head on my shoulder and we just sat there.

"What are thinking about, Jack?"

"The first time you ever told me you loved me."

"Are you still just as happy?"

"No."

"What do you mean, no? I'll kick your butt."

"I think we should go in the house, and get the pillows out."

"I'm game. That kind of statement means war."

"You didn't let me finish."

"I suggest you do it now or...."

"No, I'm not as happy now. Every since that night, my love for you has grown with more passion and strength. More than I ever thought possible. It's still growing. I can't explain it, but I do know this. You are more beautiful than the day I met you. Now that you're carrying our baby, you seem to radiate like the sun. There's a twinkle in your eyes that wasn't there before. I can hardly wait...."

"I think we should make love, Jack."

"I think you're right."

And we did. Then we fell asleep holding each other.

31

AS THE CONVERSATION CONTINUED between Michelle and Willie after we left the party, Michelle had no way of knowing that she was putting Gabriella and me in danger.

"Michelle, Gabriella sure got sick all of a sudden. Did she say anything to you?" Willie asked.

"No, honey. We were just sitting there talking, and we got up to come over to you guys, and she started feeling sick."

"Well, if that's the way you're gonna be when you get pregnant, I think I'll just move out until it's born," Willie said laughing.

"Are you saying that you want me pregnant?"

"Well, I think I'm just a little jealous of Jack and Gabriella."

"All you have to do is marry me, and I'll be glad to have your baby."

"Are you proposing or what?"

"No...You're going to do that..."

"I will real soon."

"You've been saying that for six months."

"I'll tell you what I'll do. When you're ready to give up your career and be the mother of my children, we'll get married."

"Are you serious?"

"You just say the word."

"I'm ready, Willie."

"OK, then. Michelle, will you marry me?"

"Yes."

"Are you sure you're ready?"

"I'm positive. I've been ready for a long time. You just never asked."

"Then we need to start making plans."

"I can't wait to tell my mother and father. They will be so excited."

"What do you mean, they? I thought your father was in Florida and you'd never seen him."

"Well, I thought he was until I ran into someone I thought looked like him, and it turned out to be him."

"Do I get to meet him?"

"You already have."

"When?"

"When he moved to town."

"OK, do I have to keep guessing or are you going to tell me who he is?"

"Willie, you have to promise me that you won't say anything to him until I say it's OK?"

"Michelle, why does it matter?"

"Willie!"

"All right, I promise. Now who is it?"

"Jack."

"Jack?"

"Yes, Jack."

"No way, Michelle."

"Do you think I'd make something like this up? I would have told you sooner, but I promised him I wouldn't say anything to anyone yet."

"Why did he want to keep it a secret?"

"He wanted time to explain it to Gabriella."

"How long did that take?"

"I'm not sure when he told her, but she and I talked about it at the party."

"When were you going to tell me?"

"As soon as Jack said it was OK."

"Why did you decide to tell me tonight and not wait?"

"Since we're getting married, and I already opened my big mouth, I knew it wouldn't really matter one way or the other to you."

"I just wish you had told me sooner."

"Why?"

"I just need to know these things. He and I do business together, that's all."

"Please don't say anything."

"I won't. Why don't you go on up to bed? I have a few calls to make, and then I'll be up. OK?"

"You won't be long, will you?"

"No. I just need to get these calls done tonight."

She left the room and Willie walked over to his desk, dialed a number and began talking, "Bill, call me now," and he hung up the phone.

32

THE ICE TRAY WAS SITTING ON THE NIGHT STAND, and Bill reached over and took out another cube. As he leaned back over Sandy, he put the ice cube in his mouth. She had her eyes closed as he began to kiss her neck and the ice slowly melted from within his mouth. Just as it seemed she couldn't stand any more, he raised his head momentarily, then continued downward.

"Bill, I can't stand this anymore. Come up here and make love to me."

Bill didn't even stop to look up as he continued over her breast, slowly working the ice in and out of his mouth. She was moaning softly as he reached her belly button. He let the cold water drip into the small cavern and then sucked it out. She moaned again.

"Bill, no more. I mean it."

"Sandy, shut up," Bill shouted and he lowered his head again. He was getting closer and closer to the spot that she had wanted him to be all night. Just as he reached the hairline between her legs, his pager went off.

"Bill, call me now," were the words he heard Willie say.

"Don't you dare stop, Bill," Sandy almost yelled.

He continued through her hair until he felt the moisture from the inside of her seeping out. At that point he swallowed what was left of the ice cube and continued kissing and enjoying the juices that were escaping from within her.

Suddenly, Bill raised up and looked at Sandy. "I hate to do this, but I have to make a call. Can you hold that thought for a minute?"

"Bill, I'm going to kick your ass."

"I'll only be a minute."

He sat up and dialed Willie's number. "What's up, boss?"

"Get your ass over here, now!"

"Willie, I'm in bed."

"Listen, we may have a problem with Jack. I need to talk to you now."

33

WILLIE, YOU'RE NOT GOING TO LIKE WHAT I FOUND OUT about Jack," Bill said. Bill had been sent out to dig up some background on Jack.

"I had a feeling that something was wrong with him the minute Michelle said he was her father. OK, what's the problem?"

"Jack Cannon is really Jack Kincaid. He was an accountant who worked in Florida. About eight years ago he turned in some dealers down there, and more than thirty of them went to prison. There was a contract out on him, and he was supposedly killed about nine months ago in Colorado. I guess they didn't do the job."

Willie's face turned red with anger. His eyes narrowed as he began to speak, "Bill, are you sure?"

"Without a doubt. Here's a picture."

Willie held the picture for a minute and just stared at it. The anger began to grow even more. He walked around the living room for a few minutes, just staring at the picture. Finally he turned to Bill and spoke in a very calm voice. "I'm going to kill that son of a bitch. That motherfucker is setting me up. I know he is."

Again, Willie walked around the room. "Bill, I want you to get in touch with all our people and tell them it's time for us to move. Transfer all my money to the new accounts, and have the jet ready tonight. Got that?"

"Sure Willie."

"As soon as that son of a bitch leaves for work, I want you to bring me his wife. I'll get that motherfucker."

"You want his wife...."

"That's what I said. I'll get to him through her. Nobody fucks with me and gets away with it."

"Where do you want me to take her, Willie?"

"Take her to the plane and wait. I'll be there later. Now, go upstairs and bring Michelle down here."

Bill left the room without another word. Willie walked over to the windows that looked out over his estate and stared. The fire was burning in his eyes, and his mind was busy at work. It was only a matter of a few minutes before Bill returned with Michelle and they entered the room.

"Good morning, Willie," Michelle said as she walked over to Willie and gave him a kiss on the cheek.

Without a word to Michelle, Willie turned around and spoke to Bill, "Take care of that shit now, and let me know when you're done."

"It won't take long. I'll call from the jet."

Willie turned back to Michelle and said, "Sit down, we have to talk."

"What's wrong, Willie?"

"Michelle, sit down."

She walked to the sofa and sat down. Willie walked around the room again and finally stopped in front of the fire place. The anger raged in his body.

"That motherfucking father of yours is working for the feds. He plans on turning me in to them."

"For what Willie?"

"Michelle. Don't you have any idea what I do to make all this money?"

"Not really. I didn't think it was any of my business. Are you in trouble with the law or something? I have some friends...."

"Don't be stupid, Michelle. You can't help. Besides, I can take care of this myself."

"What has my father got to do with this?"

"He turned a bunch of guys into the feds down in Florida. That's why he has a new name, Michelle. That's what he was going to do to me. Do you understand me now?"

"Willie, are you in that much trouble?"

"No....I'm not in any trouble. Jack is in trouble. No...let me correct that. Jack's trouble will soon be over."

"Willie, what are you going to do?"

"Michelle, you have to understand. Jack fucked me over and no one gets away with that."

"Willie, he's my father."

"Michelle, you barely know the man. The question I put to you now is, do you love me or not?"

"Of course, I love you. That's a dumb question."

"Then you have to understand what I have to do. All I can say is that Jack Kincaid is a dead man."

34

GABRIELLA, I'LL CALL YOU AS SOON AS I TALK TO SANDY."

We were standing at the door as I was leaving for the campus. She had decided to take a cab to work so that I could see Sandy before classes.

"Jack, be careful. I love you so very much."

"Don't worry, Gabriella. Everything will be just fine. I promise."

"I love you," and she threw her arms around me and we held each other very close for a long time. Finally I tore myself away from her. I could tell she was very worried, and I had to get her out of this mess that I had created. I got in my car and drove off.

This had gotten totally out of hand and I had to get Sandy to get us out of here. I continued down the main strip of town with the radio blaring as I thought about the safety of the woman I loved, and the child she carried inside her. Our child. We wanted this baby so much. It was to be the final piece of the puzzle that made our paradise complete. I was jeopardizing that and I was going to straighten it out today. Sandy would get us out. Today.

My pager went off. I looked at the message indicator. It read "143-1012-334." It was from Gabriella. The "143" meant that she was saying "I Love You," the "1012" was the radio station that we always listened to when a favorite song came on, and "334" stood for "You are mine." I turned up the radio and heard a song by Celine Dion. The words sang out, "I am Your Lady and You are My Man..." She had sung this song to me many times. I felt tears come to my eyes as I continued to drive. I knew beyond a shadow of a doubt that this woman loved me as much as I did her when she sung it to me. She would hold my hand and look at me with those beautiful brown eyes and just sing. I loved her for the passion and heart she added to the song. Beyond the words, "I am Your Lady and You are My Man," the other lyrics didn't matter. What mattered was, I knew that she loved me as much as I loved her.

I pulled the car over at the next pay phone I saw, and wiped the tears from my eyes as I dialed her pager number. I simply put, "334-69-143-2" as the message.

I went straight to Sandy's apartment and knocked on the door.

"Jack, I'm glad you're here. I think we might have a problem."

"Sandy, I'm *sure* we have a problem."

"What happened?"

"It's kind of a long story and I should have told you as soon as I found out, but I thought I could handle it."

"Well, let me tell you what happened last night. Bill was here and Willie paged him. Bill called him back and I overheard your name. Bill looked very startled and left right after that. It had something to do with you, I'm sure."

The blood in my body moved at breakneck speed to my head. I felt all the pressure in my face. "I was sure she wouldn't say anything."

"She who, Jack? What's going on?" Sandy screamed.

"Michelle."

"What about Michelle?"

"She's my daughter."

"She's your what?" Sandy screamed again. "Why didn't you tell me?"

I began to tell Sandy the whole story. It took about half an hour and two cups of coffee. She looked more and more worried as I continued. When I finished, she looked at me and I knew what she was going to say before she opened her mouth, "Jack, you should have told me. This ends the whole operation. We have to clean out now. I'm going to call Cheryl and Gary and get them over here. As soon as they get here, I want you and Cheryl to go get Gabriella. Then I want you all back here. Pronto. Do you understand."

"Of course I understand, Sandy," I yelled. "I'm as worried as you are."

"I'm sorry, Jack. We have to do this and do it fast, before it's too late."

Cheryl and Gary were there within fifteen minutes, and five minutes later Cheryl and I were on our way.

"Cheryl, we better go by the bank first and see if she's there yet. What time do you have?"

"It's 10:15."

"Yeah, she should be there now."

We parked the car and went into the bank. She wasn't there. I went to one of the courtesy phones and dialed our number. There was no answer. She must be on her way. She was always late.

"Jack, let's head to the house and we'll catch her in the cab."

"OK, Cheryl."

We drove toward the house looking for a cab of any kind heading our direction. None. Not one cab.

We pulled into the driveway, and both got out and ran into the house.

"Gabriella," I shouted. No answer. We searched the house, but she wasn't there.

"Jack, did you see her purse any where?" Cheryl asked.

"I didn't even look, Cheryl."

I ran back to the bedroom and looked on the dresser for her purse. There it sat just where she always put it.

"Cheryl, something's wrong."

"Jack, call the bank and see if she's there."

I picked up the phone and dialed the number already knowing what the answer would be. "Celeste, could I speak to Gabriella?" Celeste was Gabriella's supervisor.

"Jack, she hasn't made it in yet. I was just going to call your house."

"Thanks, Celeste. I'll call you as soon as I can." And hung up the phone.

"Jack, call the hospital. She might have gotten sick," Cheryl suggested.

"OK," I said, but I already knew the answer. They hadn't had a Mrs. Cannon this morning.

"Now what, Cheryl?" My body was dying. "I'll call Sandy. She'll know what to do."

In a matter of minutes Sandy and Gary were there, and I could see the worried look in their eyes.

"Jack, I've already called Steve and he's on the way. Our agents are either at Willie's house already or on their way there. Don't worry Jack, we'll find her."

"Sandy, Willie's got Gabriella, I'm sure of it."

"Jack, you're not sure of anything."

"Sandy, I'm sure."

"Jack!"

"Sandy, I'll kill that son of a bitch if he hurts her at all."

"Jack, let's just wait and see."

35

WELL, I SEE YOU'VE GOT OUR FRIEND HERE, Bill," Willie said with a look of victory in his eyes.

"What's going on, Willie?" Gabriella said.

"You don't say anything, bitch, unless I ask a question."

"But Willie...."

As she said those words, Willie raised his hand and slapped her across the face, and she tumbled to a seat in the jet.

"I said don't say anything unless I ask you a question. Bill, have you made all the arrangements?"

"Everyone has been warned and they are leaving this morning. The money has all been transferred to the new accounts and everything here is being sold this morning."

"What about the stuff we just bought?"

"It's loaded on the jet with us. Everyone is to meet us in Mexico tomorrow."

"Great."

"What's next, Willie?"

"Well, we have a little business to finish here tonight and then we leave."

"OK. What do you want me to do?"

"Get that bitch over here and hold her hand out for me. The left one."

"Willie, what you going to do?" Michelle said almost in a scream.

"Michelle, you either shut the fuck up, or get the hell out of here now."

She turned and went to sit in one of the passenger seats up front. She was crying, but had quickly learned not to argue with Willie.

"Bring her over here, Bill." Willie placed her hand palm down on the table in the plane. "Bill, put your hand over her mouth." He reached in his pocket and pulled out a switchblade, flipped it open, then lowered it to her hand. Gabriella's eyes widened with horror and her body was trembling. Willie looked Gabriella in the eyes, and began to speak again, "This is just to let Jack know that I'm serious."

In one swift motion, he had Gabriella's ring finger holding it still, took the knife, and cut it off just above her wedding ring. Blood shot out everywhere. Gabriella was screaming even though it was muffled through Bill's hands. Michelle was screaming in the background, but Willie wasn't listening.

"Wrap her hand up, Bill. We don't want her to bleed to death."

He put Gabriella back in the seat and she passed out in shock.

"Michelle, get over there and look after her," Willie ordered. This is a side of Willie she had never seen.

"This is just to get Jack's attention. I'm done with her."

"Promise me, Willie," she said as the tears were running down her eyes.

"I promise, Michelle. Just take care of her. Bill, take this over and put it in their mailbox and then come right back here. If there's any problem at all, just throw it in their front yard. Then get back here. Got it?"

"No problem."

Bill wrapped Gabriella's finger in a towel and put it in one of the bags that are used when people get airsick on planes. He turned to Willie and said, "Anything else I need to do?"

"Nothing. Just get back here."

Bill drove the car to Jack's house, delivered the package and returned to the jet.

36

*I*T WAS LATE AFTERNOON NOW and I was dying. I knew that Willie had Gabriella, and our life was shattered. Why didn't he just take me or kill me? Why Gabriella? Why Gabriella? My life was over.

"Jack, we'll find them and she'll be OK. He wants something, I'm just not sure what it is yet," Sandy said.

"We'll find her Jack," Gary said.

"If only I hadn't been so stupid, this would never have happened."

"It's too late to worry about that, we just have to fix it," Cheryl said.

"I want you and Gary to go over to the campus and see if you can find out anything from Matt or any of those other assholes who are involved," Sandy commanded.

"We're on our way," Gary said.

Just as they were about to walk out the door, the phone rang.

"Hold on guys," Sandy said

I ran and grabbed the phone, "Hello?"

"Well, motherfucker. Your ass is mine."

"Willie, where's Gabriella? I'll kill you if you hurt her, you son of a bitch."

"I guess you haven't found my little package yet. Go out to your mail-box, shithead."

I placed my hand over the receiver, "Gary, the mailbox." He ran out and brought back the bag.

"Willie, I'll kill you if you lay a hand on her."

"You're not going to do anything except listen, because if you want Gabriella to live you'll do exactly as I say. Got it?"

My body died. He was in control and I knew it.

"All right Willie. What do you want?"

"Tonight at nine o'clock, I want you to come to the parking lot of the stadium. I want you alone. No cops, no feds. No one. I'll let Gabriella go and you come with me. If you screw up at all, Gabriella's dead. Got it?" Willie commanded.

"Done...I want to talk to Gabriella."

"Fuck you....You just be there," and he hung up the phone.

I turned around and saw Sandy, Gary, and Cheryl huddled around the table. Sandy and Cheryl were both in tears. I walked over to the table, and there on the towel was Gabriella's finger.

I felt a knot in my throat and trembled as I screamed, "Oh my God! That son of a bitch is dead. Either he kills me or I'll kill him."

"Jack, what did he say?" Sandy asked.

I went through the whole thing again crying, and trying to keep my composure.

When I was finished I said to Sandy, "I want a .45 to carry with me."

"We'll have people in the stadium. I'll get it arranged now."

"Sandy, I don't think you understand. No one is going to be there but me."

"Jack, he'll kill you and probably Gabriella, too."

"If you guys are there, he'll kill her for sure. No...I don't want anyone there. I think I'll have a better chance."

"Jack!"

"Sandy. End of discussion."

"OK, Jack. At least let one of us hide in the car to make sure she gets away from them, if the exchange goes through. She might be real weak."

"Only if you promise not to interfere."

"Promise. I'll just drive her away from there."

"So, I guess the someone will be you."

"I want to be there if it's all right with you."

"Only if you don't interfere."

"I just want to make sure she gets out, I promise."

"Get me the gun, Sandy."

"You'll have it."

37

AT ABOUT 8:30, I PULLED OUT OF THE GARAGE and headed toward the campus. My heart was beating so fast that I thought I might lose control. Sandy was on the floor of the car and wasn't saying a word. All I could think about was making sure that Gabriella was safe. I couldn't believe things had gotten so screwed up so quickly. What a fool I had been.

I thought about that first time we really made love and how wonderful it was. How beautiful she was lying on the bed next to me. How exhausted we were and how happy we were. The little personal things we said to each other, and how every word that we spoke seemed to be what God had brought us together for. Through us, God had a plan, and I knew it couldn't end like this.

I pulled into the stadium parking lot and started looking for some sort of car. At the far end of the stadium I saw Willie's limousine. I slowly moved my car in same direction.

"Willie's limo is sitting at the far end of the parking lot."

"Do you see anything else?"

"Nothing."

"Be careful, Jack. And good luck."

"You just get Gabriella out of here."

"I'll do it."

"About another hundred yards."

I slowly pulled the car to a stop about fifty feet from his limo, turned off the engine and the headlights. I wanted to give myself time to get used to the darkness. His windows were tinted and I couldn't see anyone inside. I didn't have to wait long.

Willie slid out of the passenger side of the front set, and pulled Gabriella out at the same time. I couldn't see anyone behind the wheel. He stepped a few feet away from the limo, and threw Gabriella to her knees. He had her hands tied behind her back and her mouth was taped.

"OK, asshole. Start walking this way," he commanded.

As I started walking, Gabriella raised her head to look at me. Her beautiful brown eyes were so sad. I had to kill this man.

"That's far enough, Jack," and I stopped. He pulled a gun from his pocket and continued to talk as he pointed it at her head, "Now, I'll show you what I do to fuckers like you who fuck up my operation."

"You said you'd let her go, Willie. I'm alone and unarmed."

"Well, motherfucker, I lied. First I want you to watch her die, and then it's your turn."

He cocked the trigger on the 357 magnum he had in his hand. I didn't even hear the door of the limo open.

"Willie, you promised you wouldn't hurt her," Michelle screamed.

"Get back in the car, Michelle," he said as he turned slightly to respond to her.

I reached for the gun I had in back of my pants, but it was too late.

"Willie, you promised," Michelle screamed again. Tears running down her eyes. She raised a gun that she had at her side. "Willie, I can't let you do this."

"Michelle, get back in the car." He turned back toward me, and saw that I was reaching for the gun.

"Too late, motherfucker."

Two shots rang out almost simultaneously. I saw Gabriella fall to the ground. Willie turned toward Michelle. She pulled the trigger again. Willie fell to the ground dead.

I ran to Gabriella. There was blood on the ground under her head. She was still breathing, but unconscious. I untied her hands, took the tape from her mouth and had her on my lap almost in one motion.

I yelled at Sandy, who was already out of the car, "Call an ambulance, Sandy, hurry."

I started crying out of control, "Gabriella, hold on. Please darling hold on, I love you. Be strong, please...."

Epilogue

I am glad you guys could come over for dinner tonight. Gabriella was looking forward to this. It's been quite awhile since we were all together," I said as I was setting the table.

"It's been three-and-a-half years, Jack," Sandy said.

"That's too damn long, my friend," Gary said.

"How's your work going, Jack?" Cheryl asked.

"You know me, I always enjoyed teaching."

"Where's Gabriella?" Sandy asked.

"She isn't feeling very well. She said she would come down later. I told her to get some rest and if nothing else, she could see you guys tomorrow."

"I hope she's OK," Cheryl said.

"Oh, she'll be fine. Well, let's eat," I said.

Gabriella's cold had been hard on her, and she slept through dinner.

We talked about old times and what they had been doing these many years. Cheryl and Gary had gotten married. Sandy was now the head of the whole east coast FBI. They were all doing great. About midnight they decided to excuse themselves.

"Jack, be sure and tell Gabriella we love her, and that we'll see her tomorrow," Sandy said.

"Yes, for us, too, Jack," Cheryl said.

"She'll be so happy to see you guys."

They got in their car and drove off into the night. I stood at the door for a few moments reflecting back on that night at the stadium's parking lot. All the ambulances, police cars, the noise, and Gabriella lying there on the ground. I slowly closed the door and walked through the house turning off the lights. I quietly made my way up the stairs and tiptoed over to the bed where Gabriella lay sleeping. I leaned down and gently kissed her on the forehead.

"I love you, my darling."

As I did this, she opened her big brown eyes to look up at me. She threw her arms around me and kissed me on the cheek.

"I love you, Daddy. I'm sorry I slept so long."

"You needed your rest, Gabriella. We have a big day tomorrow. Uncle Gary, Aunt Sandy and Cheryl said to tell you they love you."

"Oh, I can hardly wait to see them, Daddy."

"I know, baby."

"Daddy?"

"What, honey"

"Tell me about Mommy and God again."

"OK, but afterwards you have to promise me you'll go back to sleep."

"I promise, Daddy."

"When your mommy was hurt, way before you were born, God took care of her. She and God are sleeping now and as soon as she's well again, God will wake her up and she'll come home to us."

"Do you think she hears us when we talk to her, Daddy?"

"Gabriella, she hears every word. I promise."

"Even when I whisper 1-4-3...Daddy?"

"Even then, baby."

With that Gabriella closed her eyes, and I sat there and watched as she went back to sleep. She looked just like her mother. The woman I love....

About the Author

JON BALLARD, A VIETNAM VETERAN, has been a professor of accounting and business for the past ten years. He is currently Department Chair for the Business Administration and Computer Information Sciences departments at Tampa Technical Institute in Tampa, Florida. He is also the editor of the quarterly newsletter published at the college.

Jon has won several awards in his chosen profession,including being honored as "Teacher of the Year" on three occaisions, most recently in January 1997.

His love for teaching is equaled only by his love for writing.